"You're sure your ex isn't the one harassing you?"

"Absolutely. He left after I told him about the baby. As far as I'm concerned, good riddance."

"He's a fool" was all Jackson dared say. If he had opened up and told her everything he was thinking, she would have been even more embarrassed.

There was a strong sense of honor and righteousness in him. Always had been. Maybe that was why this police job seemed to fit him so well. Why he felt such an undeniable obligation to step up and take care of Nicolette when her need was so great. She would never know how deeply, how personally, her plight affected him, of course, because he would never tell her.

But he would be there for her, helping and guarding her to the best of his ability, for as long as she needed him to be. It wasn't only because she might help the department solve a difficult case, either.

Looking after her was simply the right thing to do.

Whether she liked it or not.

TEXAS K-9 UNIT:

These lawmen solve the toughest cases with the help of their brave canine partners

Books by Valerie Hansen

Love Inspired Suspense

*Her Brother's Keeper
*Out of the Depths
 Deadly Payoff
*Shadow of Turning
 Hidden in the Wall
*Nowhere to Run
*No Alibi
*My Deadly Valentine
    "Dangerous Admirer"
 Face of Danger
†Nightwatch
 The Rookie's Assignment
†Threat of Darkness
†Standing Guard
 Explosive Secrets

Love Inspired Historical

 Frontier Courtship
 Wilderness Courtship
 High Plains Bride
 The Doctor's Newfound Family
 Rescuing the Heiress

Love Inspired

*The Perfect Couple
*Second Chances
*Love One Another
*Blessings of the Heart
*Samantha's Gift
*Everlasting Love
 The Hamilton Heir
*A Treasure of the Heart
 Healing the Boss's Heart

*Serenity, Arkansas
†The Defenders

VALERIE HANSEN

was thirty when she awoke to the presence of the Lord in her life and turned to Jesus. In the years that followed, she worked with young children, both in church and secular environments. She also raised a family of her own and played foster mother to a wide assortment of furred and feathered critters.

Married to her high school sweetheart, she now lives in an old farmhouse she and her husband renovated with their own hands. She loves to hike the wooded hills behind the house and reflect on the marvelous turn her life has taken. Not only is she privileged to reside among the loving, accepting folks in the breathtakingly beautiful Ozark mountains of Arkansas, she also gets to share her personal faith by telling the stories of her heart for all the Love Inspired Books lines.

Life doesn't get much better than that!

EXPLOSIVE SECRETS

VALERIE HANSEN

HARLEQUIN® LOVE INSPIRED® SUSPENSE

Special thanks and acknowledgment to Valerie Hansen
for her contribution to the Texas K-9 Unit miniseries.

PLEASE RECYCLE
THIS PRODUCT IS RECYCLABLE

Recycling programs
for this product may
not exist in your area.

™ LOVE INSPIRED BOOKS

ISBN-13: 978-0-373-67553-1

EXPLOSIVE SECRETS

I will give you a new heart
and put a new spirit within you.
—*Ezekiel* 36:26

To my "partners in crime,"
Shirlee McCoy, Margaret Daley, Sharon Dunn,
Terri Reed and Lenora Worth, who were a joy
to work with on this series. To Joe and Karen,
beloved proofreaders who catch my boo-boos.
And to my personal K-9 cops, Charlie Brown and Lucy,
two rescued Labs who see to it that
I don't spend every waking hour sitting at my computer.

ONE

Nicolette Johnson was about to leave for her night-shift job at The Truck Stop Diner when her cell phone rang.

She slipped it out of her jeans pocket and hesitated while she listened to the ringtone playing "The Yellow Rose of Texas." Most of her recent callers had been nosy reporters or curious neighbors wanting to ask what she knew about her cousin Arianna Munson's recent murder.

"That would be *nothing,* just like I told the police," she muttered. But since her curiosity was aroused, she gave in and answered. "Hello?"

"Hello, Nicki, darlin'."

The slow, deep drawl was dripping with menace, sending chills up her spine. "Who is this?"

"Never mind who I am. You need to stop holding out on us," the man warned. "Remember, we know where you live."

Nicki swallowed past the lump in her throat.

"I don't know what you're talking about. Leave me alone."

"That's not going to happen, lady. That idiot Murke blew it the other night, but we can still get to you, just like we got to the Serpent."

"Who?" She rued the telltale tremor in her tone.

"Arianna Munson." He gave an evil-sounding chuckle. "That was our pet name for your dearly departed cousin."

There was a pause while the caller laughed as if he'd just told a great joke. "We eliminated her, and we can do the same to you. If you think you can run or hide, just ask the Sagebrush cops what happened to one of their wives a few years back." He chortled again then shouted, *"Boom!"*

Stifling a tiny shriek, Nicki immediately ended the call. Many of the specifics of the man's threats had already become a confusing muddle, but one fact stood out. The way he had barked *boom* left no doubt that she was dealing with a deadly enemy, one she should not try to defeat on her own.

Shaking, Nicki managed to punch in the phone number from the business card the police officers had left with her a few days before. She held her breath and counted the number of rings while she waited for someone to answer.

"Sagebrush Police Department. How may I help you?" a friendly sounding woman asked.

Nicki had intended to report the sinister warning calmly and with little emotion. When she heard the dispatcher's voice, however, she blurted, "I need help. Somebody just threatened to blow me up!"

"K-9 unit 463, your position?" the patrol radio broadcast.

Jackson Worth keyed the mic. "Sagebrush Boulevard and Main, headed north."

"We have a possible bomb threat at 3274 Lost Woods Road, apartment 210. See the woman."

"Affirmative. On my way. ETA approximately ten."

"Copy. Advise if you need backup."

Jackson flipped on his light bar and spun the wheel of the SUV. In the backseat, his black Labrador retriever, Titan, was panting rapidly, knowing they were about to go to work.

The big dog's enthusiasm made Jackson smile. They were so much a team it was as if Titan could read his mind. He could certainly tell what that dog was thinking. When they were on duty his canine partner was all business, even when he acted as though he was still battling the negative effects of their previous assignments in war zones.

"We both came through the fire okay then, didn't we, old boy?" Jackson said affectionately. "And we're still doing it."

Titan wiggled, but remained disciplined enough

to stay seated and not fight the restraints that kept him safe when he wasn't riding in his portable kennel. Jackson hated to cage the tractable dog so he used every excuse not to.

They pulled to the curb in front of the apartment building on Lost Woods Road, and stopped. Jackson barely had a chance to climb out when a slim, young woman in jeans and a pink T-shirt raced over and grasped his sleeve. Her wide eyes were as blue as a summer sky, and her coppery-brown hair fell softly around her face, its silky length brushing her shoulders.

"Are you the party who placed the call for police assistance?" Jackson asked.

"Y-yes. I thought they'd send the same officers who were here before."

He politely touched the brim of his cap, then opened the rear door to leash Titan as he explained, "I'm Detective Worth, ma'am. You must have mentioned a bomb threat when you contacted the station or they wouldn't have sent us."

"I did. That's really the only thing I can remember clearly. The man who called me said I should ask about a policeman's wife getting blown up and then he hollered, *'Boom!'* Just like that." She tried to catch her breath. "I didn't know what else to do so I called the number on the card those other officers left when they were here a few days ago."

"You did the right thing by waiting outside, Ms…"

"Nicolette Johnson." She pointed to the upper story of the poorly maintained apartment building. "That's where I live. I was about to leave for work. After I got the threatening phone call, I didn't know what to do."

Jackson straightened with Titan at his side. "Okay. Let's start from the beginning. Tell me your version of the trouble you had here recently."

"Okay. A man broke into my apartment. I hid in the closet and called 911. When the other officers got here there was a fight and some shooting. That's when a police dog was wounded. It was awful."

Jackson nodded soberly. "I understand how upsetting that must have been. A fugitive named Derek Murke was arrested."

"Right. He was an ex-boyfriend of my late cousin, Arianna Munson. That's another reason I got scared. The man who called me today mentioned her. Only he called her a snake or something."

"You mean *Serpent?*"

Nicolette nodded, her eyes wide. "That was it. Serpent. He said that he had killed her."

"In those exact words?" Jackson knew that the Munson woman had died during a shoot-out with the police, so why would anyone claim murder as a threat? He had to make an effort to control his excitement. Any clues, no matter how obscure, that brought the department closer to finding the gang of killers and drug runners causing mayhem in and around Sagebrush were definitely top priority.

"I—I don't know. I'm sorry. I can't remember his exact words. I guess I was too scared."

Or up to your eyeballs in the whole criminal mess, he thought, keeping that notion to himself for the time being. "Suppose we get off the street and go check your apartment before we do anything else?"

"Okay." She was wringing her hands. "I feel silly causing such a fuss, but he sounded really serious about hurting me."

"Did he say why?"

"Yes. He seemed to think I was withholding some kind of information. Murke said the same thing when he held me hostage the other night."

"Are you?"

"Of *course* not. If I did know something, I'd have told the officers who arrested him." She shivered. "He's still in jail, isn't he?"

"Yes, ma'am. And he will be for a long time if I'm any judge. You don't need to worry about him coming back to bother you."

"Oh, good! What about the wounded police dog? Is she going to make it?"

"Yes. The muscle in her hind leg was torn up pretty bad, but the vet says Lexi will be back on duty in due time."

"That's a relief."

Nicolette was reaching for the outer door to the complex when Jackson stopped her. "You'd better wait while we check the premises. I'll signal you to come and unlock your apartment when we're sure the halls are clean."

She seemed reluctant. "Okay, but..."

"Just stand where we can still see each other," Jackson told her. "If Titan finds anything suspicious, he'll sit down by it, and then I'll call for backup and evacuate the building. If he doesn't react, you'll know everything is fine."

"What a beautiful, intelligent animal," she said softly as man and canine started to walk away.

Jackson watched Titan methodically check every corner and sniff at every door on the ground floor. Then they returned to Nicolette.

"Coast is clear down here. Where's your apartment?"

"Second floor, far end of the hall." She held up a key. "Do you need this?"

"Not yet. Let us take the lead. You can follow at a safe distance. When Titan is satisfied, you can come and unlock the door for us."

It would have given Jackson a better feeling if he'd had at least one more officer with him to guard the young woman, although in this case it seemed unnecessary. Whoever had tried to frighten her had succeeded, yes, but that wasn't proof of real danger. As long as Titan didn't alert, he'd be satisfied that the place was free of explosives. That was the main thing.

Finished with the second phase of the sweep, he paused at apartment number 210 and motioned to Nicolette.

Watching her hurry to join them he was taken by her grace, her natural loveliness. So many women he'd known in the past seemed to think that painting themselves up was the key to beauty. As far as Jackson was concerned, a naturally pretty woman like Nicolette Johnson was far easier on the eyes.

You're on the job. You're not supposed to notice things like that, his conscience reminded him.

That made Jackson smile slightly. He might be working. And he was certainly not in the market for romance of any kind. But that did not mean he was unable to appreciate this kind of loveliness, any more than he could overlook a gorgeous Texas sunset or the shining, coppery coat on a special chestnut-colored mare out at his ranch.

His smile threatened to widen and he had to stifle it. He could just imagine what Ms. Nicolette Johnson would think of having her beauty compared to that of a fine horse, even if it was one of the nicest compliments he could have bestowed.

Nicki's hands were trembling so badly she had trouble fitting the key into the lock. When she was finally successful, she stepped back and let the dog and his handler enter while she waited by the door.

It was interesting seeing how they worked as a team with the dog leading the way and the man indicating when he wanted him to proceed to another room.

If the apartment hadn't been so small and sparsely furnished, she would have worried more when they both disappeared into the bedroom. Thankfully, there wasn't much to see and their inspection was complete in a matter of minutes.

"You can come in and relax now," Jackson called. "The place is clean. There's no danger."

Frowning, she poked her head in first. "You're sure?"

"Titan is," Jackson said with a smile. "You can trust him. I do."

"Okay." She took a few steps closer and eyed her tiny living room. "I suppose I'd notice if there was anything out of place. It's just that the last few days have been so awful. The landlord repaired my front door after the female police officer forced it, but I thought I'd never get the stains out of my rug from where that poor dog was wounded."

"I understand your concern." He waited for her to sit in the only easy chair before taking a place across from her on the slipcovered sofa. Titan lay at his feet. "Now that we can take it easy, how about starting from the beginning and telling me what's been going on?"

Sighing, she began. "I feel like I've just run a marathon instead of sleeping 'til noon. I work nights at The Truck Stop Diner out on Highway 20 so I don't get up very early." Her stomach fluttered, then settled, much to her relief. She didn't think it was this officer's business that she was expecting a baby so she kept that information to herself.

His eyes never left her face as he asked, "I take it that's your normal schedule. Are you a waitress?"

"No. I'm one of the short-order cooks. I've worked that shift for the past year."

"How about neighbors? Any trouble with them lately?"

"No."

"Boyfriends? Anybody you may have argued with?"

Hadn't he heard a word she'd said? "I told you what the caller wanted. He knows—knew—my cousin, Arianna. That's what this is all about.

Everybody thinks she told me some secret, but she didn't."

Nodding, he seemed to be trying to stare right into her mind because his gaze was unwavering. "I'd like to believe you, but there's a problem with that," Jackson said.

"A problem? What?"

"I heard your cousin's dying declaration with my own ears. She said, 'Cousin. Code. Danger.'"

"Now you sound like Murke!" Nicki jumped to her feet and began to pace the small room. "Arianna and I were related, yes, but we weren't close. Not anymore. There's no reason for her to even mention me."

"Does she have other cousins?"

Nicolette's shoulders slumped and she shook her head slowly. "Only one that I know of. I have a half sister somewhere back East. Since even *I* don't know where she is, I'm sure Arianna couldn't have meant her."

"So, that leaves you," he said calmly.

"I know, I know." She blinked back unshed tears, unwilling to let a stranger see how close she was to losing control of her emotions. That was another of the side effects of pregnancy, or so she had read, and she couldn't believe how often she'd fought mood swings lately.

"We'll need your half sister's name." He poised to write in a small notebook.

"Her maiden name was Mae Johnson. I heard she got married. I don't know what her last name is now."

"We'll track her down, just in case." He stood and pocketed the notebook and pen. "Are you sure there's nothing else you'd like to tell me?"

"No! Nothing. I don't know why nobody will believe I'm innocent."

"It doesn't matter what I do or don't believe, Ms. Johnson. I'm just doing my job."

"I know you are. Sorry."

He nodded stiffly. "No problem. I'll be glad to escort you to work if you want."

Nicki almost told him to go away, to leave her alone and stop treating her as though she was lying. If she hadn't still been so afraid she might have done so.

"Okay. I guess there's no sense sitting home brooding," she finally said with a muted sigh. "Besides, I can't afford to make my boss mad. When I had to call in sick the other night after Murke came gunning for me, Lou told me it had better not happen again or I'd be fired."

"In that case, we should get going. If you receive more strange calls or notice anything unusual, feel free to call us again. That's what we're here for."

"Thanks." She hesitated. "Would you mind

walking me to my car and having the dog check it, too? Just in case."

"Sure. Be glad to."

Nicki grabbed her wallet off the end table and fisted her keys. They jingled, attracting the dog's attention and making him pant and wag his tail.

"Looks like your partner is ready to go for a ride."

"Titan is always ready for adventure." Jackson stepped to the side while Nicki opened the apartment door.

She halted abruptly, staring at the floor. Someone had tucked a small, fresh flower arrangement in the doorway so that she couldn't miss seeing it.

"Oh, how pretty. I love daisies."

Jackson frowned. "I thought you said you didn't have a boyfriend."

"I don't. Not since Bobby Lee got so mad and took off. Maybe he changed his mind." She bent and reached for the flowers.

To her left, she saw Titan plop down into a sitting position so fast the movement was a blur.

Jackson shouted, "No!" and lunged for her.

Half bent over, Nicki was almost toppled. She recovered, managing to rescue the bouquet by clutching it to her chest.

Titan began to bark.

In what felt like one fluid movement, Jackson

grabbed the flower arrangement from her, threw it inside the apartment, shoved her and the dog into the hall and slammed the door. Then he covered and shielded them both as best he could with his own body.

Moments later, a loud explosion shook the building and made Nicki's ears sting as if they were being stabbed by needles. Stunned, she could hardly breathe.

The flowers! She could have been killed. So could her innocent baby. But they were safe! *Thank you, Jesus.*

As the officer slowly straightened and allowed her to move, she felt so light-headed she was afraid she might faint. If she hadn't already been sitting on the floor she knew she would have been reeling.

Tears gathered and spilled down her cheeks. So utterly thankful she could not speak, she threw her arms around the dog's neck, pressed her face into his fur and silently wept as the reality of her situation dawned. There would not always be a police officer at hand to rescue her at the last second, so what could she do? What *should* she do?

Nicki was at a loss to know. Death had stalked her, and she had once again triumphed. The question was, how many more narrow escapes could she hope to endure before some lurking, unnamed evil slipped through her meager defenses and succeeded in ending her life?

TWO

"It doesn't make any sense for them to want to hurt her when they think she's keeping secrets," Jackson told Captain Slade McNeal as they stood apart from the other officers at the scene of the chaos. "If the gang wants the information Arianna gave her, they need to keep her alive and well."

"Unless they knew you were with her and figured your dog would identify the device before it was touched."

"Possibly."

"How's the woman doing?" Slade asked.

"She's scared silly. Who wouldn't be?" Jackson paused and raked his fingers through his short, dark hair. "I can't believe how close we all came to buying the farm."

"Yeah. It wasn't a big explosion, but it sure made hash out of her apartment. I'm having the paramedics hold her in the ambulance until the

ATF boys get here. They may have a few questions for Ms. Johnson, too."

"Makes me wish we had our own bomb squad right here in Sagebrush."

"Can't afford it."

"Yeah, I know. I'm just glad you hired me and Titan." He sobered even more as he regarded his superior. "We're all sorry about what motivated you."

"Thanks. I still blame myself. If you'd been here then, my wife might have been warned in time, and Caleb would still have a mother."

Chagrined, Jackson shook his head and thrust his hands into his pockets. "Don't be so sure about that. I messed up on this one."

"You saved the woman's life. I'd hardly call that a failure."

Jackson snorted derisively. "Tell that to Ms. Johnson when she gets a look at what's left of her place. It's a shambles. Every window is blown out, and the furniture looks like a wildcat on meth shredded it."

"Yeah…but she's still alive. If I were you, I'd remind her of that before I let her go up and look. The bedroom seems to have escaped damage, except for lots of plaster dust and smoke, so she will still have clothes and personal items to salvage."

"I hope that helps. She has every right to be furious with me."

"You're too hard on yourself," McNeal told him. "Why don't you go see to your dog and check on Ms. Johnson while I wait for Boomer."

"Right." Hearing the familiar ATF agent's nickname almost always made Jackson smile. Any guy with the initials TNT was a shoo-in for a bomb-investigating job. Timothy Nelson Taft was not only good at his job, he seemed to enjoy the good-natured teasing he usually received when people realized why he was called *Boomer.*

Several other members of the Sagebrush P.D. and fire department were milling around the rescue and police vehicles parked in the street. Some regular officers had cordoned off the apartment grounds and were detouring traffic. That was probably unnecessary, yet Jackson didn't complain. He had mistakenly underestimated their foes and an innocent bystander had almost paid for his laxity.

He went first to Titan and the fellow K-9 officer who was tending to him. Valerie Salgado's Rottweiler had been the one wounded on these premises a few days ago and since Valerie was on her own for the present, she had volunteered to look after Titan while Jackson spoke to their captain.

A tall woman with green eyes, freckles and

long, reddish hair, Salgado was seated in one of the SUVs, petting Titan to soothe his jangled nerves.

"How's he doing now?" Jackson asked, approaching.

"Better. He's not shaking nearly as much as he was when I got here. What happened, anyway? Didn't he alert properly?"

"The dog did fine." He reached toward his canine partner to affectionately ruffle his velvety ears. "I was the one who messed up. I let a civilian get ahead of me and she picked up the bomb before I could stop her."

"That's when it went off?"

"No, thank God. Literally. I had a few seconds to grab it and throw it. Unfortunately, the only place I could pitch it was into her apartment."

"Better a few dented walls than dented heads." She gently stroked Titan's broad back, wiggling her fingers, much to the dog's delight. "What a good boy."

"Do you have time to mind him for me a little while longer? I want to check with the EMTs and see how the vic is doing." Jackson inclined his head toward a parked ambulance.

"Sure. No sweat. I'll take him back to the station with me and you can pick him up there later, if you want. Lexi won't be able to work for a while yet, and I miss relaxing like this." She sighed. "Petting a dog lowers your blood pressure and does all kinds of good things for your state of mind."

"I know. Just save me a little Titan chilling time. I'll need it after I get through showing the lady over there what happened to her apartment."

He could hear Valerie's light laughter behind him as he started for the ambulance.

One of the paramedics headed him off before he got all the way to where Nicolette was being treated.

"Worth. Hold up," the medic said. "I need to talk to you for a sec."

"Sure." He peered past the shorter, younger man's shoulder. "Is there a problem?"

"Not yet. At least not that I know of, but you should know that this victim is pregnant before you continuing questioning her."

That brought Jackson up short. "She's okay, though? I hit her pretty hard when I was shoving her out of the way."

"Seems to be. It's early in the pregnancy so she's not showing. There's no way you'd have known unless she chose to tell you."

He huffed quietly. "I figured she was holding something back, but I had no idea that was it. No wonder she seemed so overwrought."

"Yeah, well, I wanted you to know."

Jackson clapped him on the shoulder and stepped past. "Thanks, man. I owe you one."

The ambulance was positioned at an angle to the curb so it could go into action without delay. Jackson made sure he was smiling as he circled it and came face-to-face with Nicolette.

The woman's eyes were misty as she looked up at him and asked, "Are you okay?"

"I'm supposed to be the one asking you that."

"I'm fine." She returned his smile. "Well, relatively fine."

When he said, "I'm really sorry about your apartment," he saw her face grow ashen.

"How bad is it?"

"Truthfully? It's a mess. But the good news is we're all safe and sound." Noticing that her arms were crossed to hug her torso he added, "*All* of us."

Rosy patches replaced the lack of color in her cheeks. "The medics told you?"

"About the baby? Yes. I hope I didn't hurt you when I knocked you down. I had no idea…"

"I'd lots rather be knocked over than blown to bits, so thank you for saving me—us. When I saw your dog react that way, I didn't put two and two together fast enough. If you hadn't been there…"

She raised her eyes to the apartment building. "I can't see any damage to the outside."

"It wasn't a large explosion," Jackson explained.

"I don't think they actually intended to kill you. Not if they really do think you're withholding information they need."

Nicki rolled her eyes. "I am *not*. What do I have to do to convince everybody of that?"

"I don't know that you can. Or if you should," he replied soberly. "You might be better off if the criminals keep on believing you do have info they need."

Shoulders slumped, she exhaled noisily. "Okay. What's next? How long before I can go back inside?"

"Hours, at least. The bomb crew and our local techs need to comb the wreckage. If the captain okays it and you're up to it, I suggest you go on to work for the present."

"Will that be safe?"

"You're safer in a crowd than you would be alone in that apartment." He smiled. "Besides, I plan to accompany you."

"My boss won't like it if you just hang around and watch me work. He never approved of my... Never mind."

Jackson assumed, judging by the face she was making, that she was remembering her now-absent boyfriend. How any man could abandon a woman like that, after what he'd done to her, made Jackson furious. "You're sure there's no way your ex could be the one harassing you?"

"No way. After I told Bobby Lee about the baby, he said some really awful things and insisted he never wanted to see me again." She grimaced. "I know it's not him."

"You're positive?"

"Absolutely. He packed up and left the day we argued while I was at work. Friends tell me he was headed for Dallas. Personally, I don't care where he is. As far as I'm concerned, good riddance."

"He's a fool" was all Jackson dared say. If he had opened up and told her everything he was thinking, she would have been even more embarrassed.

He'd always had a strong sense of honor, of right and wrong. Maybe that was why his job seemed to fit him so well. And why he felt such an undeniable obligation to step up and take care of Nicolette when her need was so great. She would never know how deeply, how personally, her plight affected him, of course, because he would never tell her.

But he would be there for her, helping and guarding her to the best of his ability, for as long as she needed him to be. It wasn't only because she might help the department solve a difficult case, either.

Looking after her was simply the right thing to do.

Whether she liked it or not.

Whether she was helping the investigation or not.

During the drive to work, Nicki had visualized her poor apartment, imagining the worst. The place hadn't been much to start with, but it was hers. The landlord had just repaired the door the police had damaged when they'd burst in to arrest Murke. No telling how upset the apartment manager was going to be when he saw what had happened today. She hoped there was insurance to cover this new damage because it was bound to cost a lot more than the broken door had, and she was pretty sure the authorities were not going to pick up the tab this time.

She parked her trusty old sedan in the usual spot behind The Truck Stop Diner and paused to try to compose herself. She'd been just getting over the jitters left after Murke's attack only to have her life thrown off-kilter once again.

If the familiar police car hadn't been following close behind her all the way, she wasn't sure she'd have been able to convince herself to go ahead and report for work. But there he was, on duty as promised.

His dog was absolutely precious—so sweet-natured and friendly. Nicki smiled to herself, noting that both man and canine had the same dark, silky hair and puppy-dog brown eyes.

She looked in the car's mirror and fastened her long hair out of the way as her job required. Two quick twists of an elastic band and she was good to go. "I can do this," she told herself. "I've worked here so long I could fill the orders in my sleep."

A smile lifted one corner of her mouth as she climbed out of her car, locked it and pocketed the key ring. Considering her lack of adequate sleep since Murke's break-in, and the adrenaline she had expended today, she just might doze off at the grill. The books she'd read about pregnancy had said to expect changes in her metabolism, but they hadn't told her how tired she'd be. Of course, those writers hadn't allowed for repeated attacks and terrifying threats, either.

Nicki glanced over to the visitor section of the lot where Jackson was parking the police car, then started for the back door leading to the kitchen. Wafting odors of burnt grease and accumulated garbage overflowing the trash receptacle instantly set her stomach churning.

Seeking to escape the cloying stench, she held her breath and chose a roundabout route instead of heading straight for the door.

A shadowy figure, hardly more than a blur, appeared for an instant in her peripheral vision. If she had continued along her usual path without diversion they could have collided!

Startled, Nicki shrieked. Whirled around. Started to run without waiting to see who or what had scared her.

A dark shape loomed directly in front of her. She crashed into a hard chest and would have fallen if the man had not quickly grabbed and steadied her.

Clenching her fists, she began to beat on him.

"Whoa. Take it easy. It's me. It's me."

As the voice penetrated her fog of fear, she realized it was familiar. Gasping, she looked up at Jackson Worth and managed to croak out, "Somebody tried to grab me!"

"Are you sure? Where? I didn't see a thing."

"Back by the trash bin." She struggled to catch her breath.

Bright lights twinkled at the corners of her eyes. Her head spun. Her legs refused to support her.

She could sense that she was being lifted and cradled protectively just as the parking lot vanished and blackness wrapped her like a warm blanket.

Fighting was useless. Surrender felt too good.

Bearing his lightweight burden, Jackson shouldered through the front door of the main service station complex and carried Nicki past racks of cellophane-wrapped snack food and into the dining area. Their passage generated a few raised eyebrows but apparently his uniform, badge and gun were enough to keep any of the truckers or other customers from interfering.

As she began to stir, she slipped an arm around his neck, laid her cheek on his chest and clung to him as if she knew what she was doing. That was troubling. So was his reaction. Having her show such reliance felt far too good. It was also something he could not permit. He'd learned the hard way that romance and being a cop did not mix.

He lowered her to sit on the edge of one of the green plastic booth benches, unwrapped her arm from his neck and steadied her as she regained full consciousness. Her color was wan, her eyes blinking rapidly.

When she pushed him away, he realized that her earlier actions must have been instinctive rather than an effort to sway his opinion of her. That was definitely a good sign—a point in her favor.

A chubby, uniformed waitress appeared at Jackson's elbow with a glass of ice water. He nodded as he took it from her. "Thanks."

"Is Nicki okay?" the older woman asked.

"I think so. Just got too much excitement."

"I sure hope that's all it is. Big Lou is already

complaining because she's late again. He's gonna have a cow if she can't work tonight."

Jackson turned his attention back to Nicolette as the waitress left. He bent and held out the glass of water. "Here. Drink this."

"I'm not thirsty." She tried to rise, getting only partway to her feet before she plopped back down on the spongy green seat. "Uh-oh. Still dizzy."

"Let me take you to the E.R. for a checkup. You may be feeling the effects of the blast."

"No way. If I don't work, I don't eat. I'll be fine in a few minutes." She grimaced. "Sure wish I didn't have to deal with all the strong odors in that kitchen, though. Seems like everything makes me queasy these days."

"That's normal, isn't it?"

"So they say. It's just a bummer to work around food when even the thought of it makes you sick."

Jackson had to smile at her wry expression and the way she accepted her new limitations. "I can see where that might be a drawback."

A hard tap on his shoulder diverted his attention. He straightened, instinctively resting his palm on the butt of his holstered gun as he faced the burly, stubble-chinned man who had joined them. "Yes?"

The man cocked his head toward Nicolette. "She gonna work or not?"

Nicki was quick to reply, "Of course I am, Lou."

"Then get into the kitchen. I don't pay you to sit around entertaining cops."

Jackson wanted to defend the young woman by explaining what had happened to her earlier, but figured she didn't want or need his help. It was clear from her demeanor that she was used to facing down her taciturn boss. If she wanted this Lou character to know about the threats and the explosion, she'd tell him.

"I'm going to go have a look around the parking lot," Jackson explained, "and see if I notice anything out of the ordinary. You couldn't tell what startled you?"

"No. I thought there was a funny shadow back by the trash bins. I assumed it was a man. Since you didn't see anybody, maybe there was nothing there. I have been awfully jumpy lately."

"That's understandable." He took a slow step backward. "Will you be okay or do you want me to hang around for a while longer?"

"I'm fine." Pushing away from the worn, Formica-topped table, she swiveled and stood next to the booth. A relieved smile spread across her face and she held out her arms. "See? Perfect. Not dizzy at all."

"Good. I'll be in the neighborhood. Just call if you need help again and be sure to let us know when you're ready to go home. We'll have an officer stop by to escort you." Jackson eyed the portly man in the stained apron, bid him a terse "Good day" and turned to go.

He was halfway to the exit before he glanced back. The man called Lou was in the lead.

Head held high, back straight, Nicolette followed him through a swinging, half door into the busy, steamy kitchen.

Jackson paused. Found himself wishing he could help her more. But how? As things stood, it was highly likely that she was embroiled in her cousin's confusing transgressions whether she knew it or not. Therefore, unless she could prove that she and Arianna had had no contact at all, she was going to continue to be of interest to many folks.

On both sides of the law.

If she'd thought her life was complicated before, she was probably going to discover that her ordeal was just beginning.

THREE

Nicolette tried to breathe shallowly as she entered the crowded, overheated kitchen. Steam rose from stainless-steel pots simmering on the stove, and filled the air with pungent odors.

A tall, thin guy she didn't recognize was standing at the grill, flipping burgers. Judging by how stained his apron was, he'd been there for some time.

Grabbing a clean, white apron from a waiting stack, she slipped the top loop over her head, crossed the strings in the back and tied them in front at her waist.

Her eyes met Lou's. She nodded toward the man at the grill. "Who's that?"

"My sister's boy." His graying eyebrows arched as he gave her the once-over through rheumy eyes. "Had to get him to fill in for you a couple of nights ago and he worked out real good. What's wrong with you, anyways? You look kinda peaked."

"I'm fine," Nicki insisted. "Just had a really rough morning." She swallowed hard, fighting the stomach upset that kept sneaking up on her. Pregnancy wasn't predictable the way she'd assumed it would be. There seemed to be no way to avoid occasional waves of nausea, yet at other times her mood might soar for no apparent reason.

"Life ain't easy for any of us, missy. You man the grill while my nephew takes his break," Lou ordered.

"Okay. No problem." Nicki said it automatically. Only she was not okay. Not even close. Her stomach was roiling, and she wondered how long she was going to be able to control herself.

The new cook started to pass her the spatula.

Nicki reached for it, noticed it was dripping with yellowed, half-congealed grease. *Uh-oh.*

Spinning, she raced for the ladies' room.

Lou was waiting in the hallway when she finally emerged. His hairy, tattooed forearms were folded across his chest and he was glaring at her. "Well?"

"I just needed a quick break, myself, that's all."

"Tell you what," he drawled. "You can have a long break. A permanent one, starting now. You're fired."

"But…"

The man already had his back to her.

"Wait, please, Lou. I need this job."

He turned and gave her a once-over. "Yeah? So why were you late again today?"

"There was trouble in my neighborhood this morning. I had to stay until the cops said I could leave."

"Okay...suppose I buy that. How come you keep complaining you're sick all the time?"

"Not all the time. Honest. I just can't help it." Hoping the truth about her pregnancy would soften his heart she blurted out, "I'm going to have a baby."

"Uh-huh. That's what I figured. Like I said, you're done here. Pick up your final check on Friday."

"No, please. How am I going to survive?"

"Should of thought of that before you messed around and got caught."

Left alone in the dingy hallway, Nicki leaned against the wall. She felt as drained as if she'd just run a marathon. What was she going to do now? Her bills were already steep, thanks to her conniving former fiancé, Bobby Lee Crawford, and his liberal use of her credit cards without her knowledge. She was behind in the rent, too. Not to mention how expensive it was going to be to repair the damage she imagined had been done to her apartment and her furniture. Those repairs were likely to cost a lot more than she had in the bank, which was pretty much nothing.

Untying the apron, she wadded it into a ball and threw it onto a chair as she stomped out of the truck stop. What a day this had already been. She could hardly wait to see what other disheartening surprises awaited her.

This was *not* how life was supposed to be when a person became a Christian, was it? She had no idea but she was certainly going to ask Pastor Eaton the next time she saw him. Instead of life getting easier, it seemed as if her problems had become a lot more complicated since she'd turned to Jesus for help, asked for forgiveness and surrendered to the Lord a month ago.

So, now what? Nicki wondered. What, indeed? She was without a job, had no savings and was still two months in arrears on her rent because she'd believed Bobby Lee when he'd taken the cash from her and lied about paying the landlord. What a blind fool she'd been where that smooth-talking Romeo was concerned.

Her hand rested at her waist and she sighed. "Poor little baby. You sure picked a mama with her share of problems, didn't you?"

Now that she was outside in the fresh south Texas air and sunshine, she took a few deeper breaths and began to feel better. Yes, she was in a pickle because she'd trusted the wrong man with her heart, but she was strong and smart and resilient. She'd had to be to have survived thus far. There were other jobs, other cafés.

She'd never consider applying at Arianna's place, even if her cousin were still alive to give her a job, but there was the Sagebrush Diner and even the Youth Center. They might need a good cook or kitchen assistant. As long as she could ventilate the work area, she should be fine. She wasn't trained for any other decent-paying jobs, and as soon as her pregnancy started to show, she knew she'd have an even harder time finding steady work.

Determined to start looking immediately, Nicolette rounded the corner and stopped dead in her tracks. Shading her eyes, she squinted in disbelief.

There sat her car, her only means of transportation, with all four tires totally flattened!

Jackson's pager went off just as he got back to the station and reclaimed Titan.

With the dog trotting happily at his side, he headed for Slade McNeal's office to find out what was up.

"You wanted to see me, Captain?"

"Yeah. What kind of shape was the Johnson woman in when you left her?"

"Pretty good, considering." Jackson's hand rested on Titan's silky black head and he absently ruffled the dog's ears as he continued. "She thought she'd seen somebody coming after her behind the truck stop, but I didn't find anything odd when I checked that area. Why?"

"Because she just called to report that her tires had been flattened. I asked her if they'd been slashed but she didn't know. She apparently took one look and hightailed it down the road before she used her phone." He cleared his throat. "Says most of her personal belongings are still locked in the car, and she's not going back there for any reason until you show up to keep her company."

"Me?" Jackson could tell he was coloring but chose to pretend otherwise. "Why me? Was there another bomb threat?"

"No. Apparently you impressed her, Detective. She said she'd promised you she'd call."

Jackson scowled. "Hold on. She works nights. She shouldn't have even looked at her car 'til almost dawn. What was she doing out there now?"

"Guess you can ask her that when you see her." He checked a note on his desk, then handed it over. "You'll find her at the Jiffy-Suds car wash on Highway 20, down the block from where she works."

Jackson turned to leave, Titan at his side, when the captain added, "Give your dog a break and let him sniff around there if he wants. I know he's not a tracking dog like my Rio or Austin Black's bloodhound, Justice, but he has a good nose. A little cross-training might prove useful."

"Yes, sir."

"I suspect the Johnson woman is more scared than anything. Since she's apparently taken with you, I'll expect you to continue to cultivate her confidence and get us some answers."

"You still believe it's all connected? The murders, the drugs, the bomb, everything that's been happening in Sagebrush these past few months?"

The captain's jaw clenched. "It's entirely possible. Remember, one of our primary objectives is still to find my Rio and bring him home. Soon. Before the syndicate that kidnapped him decides to put a bullet in him—if they haven't already." He sighed heavily. "Caleb would never understand losing his best buddy for good. You can't explain things like that to a five-year-old. The poor kid's been a nervous wreck ever since Rio was dognapped."

"I'll do my best, sir," Jackson said. "How's your father doing? Any lasting effects from the beating he took back then?"

"Some. Dad's not himself, that's for sure. He still has to have nursing care at home. I wish I knew if the dognappers beat him because he tried to do the right thing and stop them from stealing Rio, or if they acted from plain meanness. Guess it really doesn't matter." He paused, pensive, before ordering, "Get going, Worth. Find out what the Johnson woman knows."

"Yes, sir," Jackson said, saluting as he took his leave.

The whole K-9 team had been searching for Rio—McNeal's multipurpose, elite German shepherd—since January, with little result. Whoever had taken the dog had obviously known exactly when to strike, assaulting the captain's elderly father, as well, and putting him in the hospital in a coma. Their K-9 unit had managed to rescue a neighborhood child who had been snatched after seeing Rio abducted, but as far as finding the dog went, they'd drawn a series of blanks.

Jackson gave his black Lab an additional pat as he loaded him into one of the unit's special SUVs. Losing a beloved partner like Titan the way McNeal had lost Rio would be devastating.

The search for Rio had had one unexpected benefit, however. It had given the police more leads to a crime syndicate operating in and around Sagebrush. Unfortunately, that discovery had also resulted in a string of violent deaths, the last being that of Arianna Munson—aka "the Serpent."

"So, what do you know about all this, Ms. Johnson?" Jackson muttered to himself. "And why won't you tell us?"

Maybe a better question would be, *How can I*

convince you to trust me? If Nicolette didn't realize she held the key to the puzzle that had gotten her cousin into so much trouble, perhaps he
could still succeed. All he'd have to do is get her
talking, and listen very carefully to everything
she revealed.

If the answer was there, he prayed he'd rec-
ognize it quickly. Before it was too late to save
Rio and before something else happened to the
Johnson woman.

There was no doubt in his mind. Someone was
out to get her. And they had nearly succeeded at
least twice, maybe more.

Nicki paced, perspiring more from anxiety
than from the warm Texas evening temperature.
She scanned passing traffic. She could see the
truck stop far in the distance, but figured as long
as she stayed near the activity at the car wash
she'd be safe enough, at least for the time being.

The approach of the distinctively lettered K-9
unit elated her so much, she couldn't help grinning. In seconds, she was standing beside the
driver's-side window.

Jackson rolled it down and leaned a bent arm
on the sill. "I hear you have another problem."

"You could say that. Somebody flattened all
my tires."

"Good thing you discovered it before dark," he said. "Why did you?"

"Why did I *what?*"

"Go outside. I didn't expect you to venture into the parking lot until you were off work. I don't suppose whoever messed with your car did, either. So, why were you out there now?"

"I was trying to go home," she replied with a grimace. "Right after you left, I started to feel sick. I told Lou why and he fired me."

"That's against the law. You can't be fired for being pregnant."

"No, but I can if I'm no longer able to work around food, and that's the only job I know. Besides, he's got his nephew working there now, and I have a feeling he was looking for a good excuse to let me go." She shrugged. "If it hadn't been that it would have been something else, like my being late for work again."

"Do you want me to have a talk with him? Explain the other problems you've been having and what held you up today?"

"Don't bother. I told him enough. Besides, it's none of Lou's business." She started to circle the black-and-white. "You can give me a lift back to my car, though, so I can show you what happened to it."

Jackson unlocked the passenger door with the flick of a switch. "Okay. Climb in."

Titan stuck his head over the back of the seat and panted in her ear while she fastened her seat belt.

"I'm glad you brought your buddy," Nicki said, tickling the dog under the chin. "I know he's not a protection dog, but I still feel safer when he's around."

"So do I. We've been partners since we were deployed in Afghanistan. Actually, Titan out-ranks me. It's customary for all the working dogs to hold a higher rank than their handlers."

"Really? How did you manage to bring him home with you when he was trained for the bat-tlefield?"

"It's a long story." In her peripheral vision she saw the man glance lovingly at the dog before he added, "Have you ever heard of PTSD?"

"Freaking out from stress? Sure."

"Well, dogs can get it, too. Titan and I were traveling in a convoy when the vehicle directly ahead of us was blown up by an improvised ex-plosive device. After that, he was never the same. He still works okay, but he's just too jumpy for military service. That's how I was able to keep him after my discharge."

Suddenly, a lot of things made sense to her. "I

get it. And you came here to Sagebrush because of that old explosion the lowlife on the phone was bragging about."

"That's part of the reason. My boss, Captain McNeal, lost his wife in that attack. When Titan and I applied for a job with the K-9 unit, he had a strong personal reason to convince the commissioners to hire us."

"That is so sad." She pointed toward her car as they drove closer. "There. See it? All four tires are flat."

"You stay here with Titan, and I'll go have a look. Since there's no hurry getting you back on the road, I want to examine the scene carefully."

"It could be just vandalism."

She watched him hesitate long enough to report his location to dispatch, then open the door and put one foot outside before saying, "I don't think this is any more random than the attacks at your apartment, Ms. Johnson. If you're smart, you won't get complacent."

Nicki knew he was right. Like it or not, she had become the target of some shady characters who apparently had ties to Arianna.

The biggest question was how in the world could she hope to convince them—and the police—that she was innocent. Clueless. Not worth bothering with.

Except for this particular officer, she added silently. Given a choice, she would just as soon have him hanging around a little while longer, at least until the threats stopped.

It wasn't sensible.

It wasn't logical.

But it was true. She felt a lot safer when he and his big, black dog were close by.

Like right now.

As far as Jackson was concerned, the pretty cook had dodged a theoretical bullet once again. If she hadn't been fired and, therefore, left work before nightfall, she could easily have become a crime statistic.

He swept the general area, checked inside her car and retrieved her personal belongings, then returned to Nicolette and Titan. They both seemed very glad to see him.

"Looks like somebody let the air out of the tires instead of slashing them, so you should be good to go as soon as we get them inflated."

"But…why would someone do this?"

"You really don't see the possibilities?"

"No."

He turned sideways in the seat to partially face her. "Okay. Here's what I think… I think somebody still believes your cousin told you something important, and they're determined to get the secret from you."

"By letting the air out of my tires? That's crazy."

"Not if it meant you'd be stranded at night, all alone, behind a building that provides plenty of cover from passing witnesses."

He could see that his frankness was making an impression with her. Judging by the paleness of her cheeks, he wondered if he'd gone too far.

Instinct told him to reach out to her, to squeeze her hand, to offer comfort. Training and experience warned against getting too friendly. Before Jackson could decide which concept to employ, his dog settled the question for him.

Titan stretched his big head over the seat and gave the frightened young woman a kiss on the cheek. The slurp was audible.

If she'd looked the least bit upset, Jackson wouldn't have laughed. However, when she squealed, "Eww," and swiped at her damp cheek with her palm, he had to chuckle. "Sorry. I think he wants you to know you're safe with us."

"Safe, maybe. Wet, too. Is he always this slobbery when he wants to show affection?"

"As a matter of fact, no," Jackson told her. "I guess he remembers you hugging him after the blast."

"It's a good thing I didn't give him any treats, too, or he'd have *drowned* me!"

Pointing at the dog Jackson ordered, "Down. Stay." And Titan plopped onto the backseat as if he'd had that pose in mind all along.

"He really is amazing," Nicki said. "I've never seen such a well-trained animal. Do you get to take him home with you at night?"

"Yes. I have a little ranch east of here where he can run around and unwind." He smiled. "Me, too."

"That's nice." Nicki paused and sighed. "So, what shall I do about my car? I'll need it if I'm going to go job hunting."

"I'll radio Arnie's Garage for a service truck. If the driver can't take care of your tires on the spot, I'll have the car delivered to you later. In the meantime, suppose you let me buy you a cup of coffee and maybe a bite to eat?"

"Not here," Nicki said quickly, eyeing The Truck Stop Diner. "Any place but here."

"Fine." He used his radio to order the roadside assistance, then started the SUV. "All set. How does the Sagebrush Diner sound?"

She smiled. "Wonderful."

"Good." *And while we're there,* Jackson mused, *we'll relax and talk about a lot of things, including what your crooked cousin may have told you.*

It didn't matter how much he happened to like this woman or how smitten his dog was with her, there was no way he could believe she didn't know more than she was willing to admit. Nobody her age could still be this naive, this innocent. Nobody.

This woman was hiding something. Something that was liable to get her killed if she didn't confess soon.

FOUR

Nicki rolled down the SUV window and let the balmy April air caress her face as the K-9 cop drove her into town. Many businesses were located on or near Sagebrush Boulevard, as was the large, redbrick church where she had so recently become a Christian.

They pulled up to the familiar storefront diner. "While I'm here, I can ask if they need a cook," Nicki said. "I need to find something that I can keep doing while I'm waiting for the baby."

Jackson rolled down the windows partway to give Titan fresh, cool air before he circled to open her door. "Isn't it going to be hard to be on your feet a lot?"

"I haven't had any problems yet. The biggest drawback at the truck stop was that tiny, stuffy kitchen."

She accompanied him to the diner and felt a rush of cool air as he opened the glass door in the brick facade. This place, too, smelled of cooking, but not in the way her former job had.

The booths along one wood-paneled wall beckoned, and she headed straight for the most distant one.

"I can't let you pay for my order," she insisted, scooting in. "This is not a date."

"Of course not."

"Good, because I don't want you to think I'm trying to take advantage of your kindness."

The astonished look on his handsome face almost made her giggle. It was ludicrous to suggest that anyone could take advantage of a man like this unless he permitted it. Still, she had to wonder why he was being so solicitous. Perhaps his motives were not as pure as hers.

As soon as Nicki had ordered a slab of apple pie à la mode and coffee she leaned back, folded her arms across her chest and spoke her mind. "Okay. Here we are. Now why did you *really* invite me?" The odd arch of one of his brows caused the beginnings of a cynical smile at the corners of her mouth. "Well?"

"I don't suppose you'll believe it was out of the goodness of my heart?"

"Nope. I've had my fill of manipulative men, particularly lately. Try telling me the truth."

"Fair enough." Leaning forward, his hands clasped atop the faux-wood table, Jackson spoke quietly. "My boss wants me to talk to you about what Arianna said with her last breath."

"You mean that ridiculous *code* thing that Murke was screaming about before the shooting started? Forget it. I don't know anything about any codes. I told you—my cousin and I hardly ever spoke. I am the *last* person she'd have shared an important confidence with."

"Okay. Suppose I buy that."

"What do you mean, *suppose?* It's the truth. I don't know a thing about her business or her criminal activities. She and I were at odds from the time we were teenagers. Arianna used to laugh at me for being too goody-goody. She made no bones about it."

"Then why would she waste her last breath warning you?"

"How should I know?" Nicki could tell from the warmth of her cheeks that she was getting upset. "Maybe she was trying to get me into trouble for the fun of it. She did that lots of times when we were kids."

"Okay." Jackson unfolded his napkin and eased back in the booth to make room for their orders. "Eat your pie and then we'll talk to the manager in case there's a chance for a job here."

"What about my poor apartment and my tires?"

"If the car isn't ready soon enough, I'll drive you home and the garage can deliver it later."

"Assuming I have a home. You haven't really told me what to expect."

"It's probably not as bad as you're envisioning." He paused to add cream to his coffee. "I didn't get a detailed look at it, but they tell me your bedroom is still in pretty good shape so you can salvage your clothes and things like that."

"Oh, spiffy. And I can sit in the middle of an exploded sofa to watch TV?"

To his credit, he winced. "No TV, I'm afraid. No windows, either."

"What? I can't even lock myself in?"

"Probably not, now that you mention it. I'll have a talk with your landlord and see about getting you moved into another unit."

"I don't want another unit. I want my home back. I want my job back. I want my *life* back."

"One step at a time. One day at a time," he said so calmly she wanted to scream.

Who did this cop think he was, lecturing her? He probably had a family and a real home. That was all she'd wanted. To belong again, the way she had once, when her parents were alive and life had been so peaceful. It wasn't fair that they had both been taken from her when she was in her teens and made her grow up overnight.

In retrospect, she could see that that desire for normalcy was what had gotten her into trouble with Bobby Lee, yet it had also ultimately led her back to church and had resulted in her recently renewed faith, so she could hardly complain. Now she understood how desperately she had needed God's forgiveness, His unconditional love. She still did. And so did her unborn baby.

They would make a family of their own some-day, just the two of them. Nicki knew she could handle being a single mother. Her fondest hope was that raising her child alone wouldn't be too hard on the little boy or girl.

It was becoming clear that the Lord had been protecting her when He'd allowed her to glimpse Bobby Lee's true character. Being deserted by a selfish liar like that had to be better than having him co-parenting their child.

The only thing she would have done differently, given another chance, was avoid listening to her biological clock and believing the sweet lies and so-called marriage proposal of that handsome cowboy-type in the first place. Anybody could look good in a Stetson. It took a special man to deserve to become a father.

The trip back to Nicki's apartment was short and uneventful. Jackson pulled up to the curb and stopped. "I truly am sorry you lost your job."

"Yeah, me, too." She sighed wearily. "I'm be-ginning to realize how hard it's going to be to find another cooking position. Sagebrush is too small."

"You'll find something. I know you will. My earlier offer stands. If you want me to speak to Lou for you, I'll be glad to."

Nicki shook her head. "No. I can't go back to work there. Just the thought of that steamy, stinky little kitchen turns my stomach."

"Okay." Jackson circled the SUV to open her door. "First things first. I'll walk you up to your apartment so you can get some of your things."

"Then what? I have no place to go."

"There must be an empty suite close by, hopefully in this same building." He saw she was standing strong, unwavering. Nevertheless, he felt it would do her good to have Titan along so he also leashed the dog and let him jump down. "Let's stop at the manager's unit on the way up and ask."

"Whatever you say. I'm beyond logical thought right now. It seems like my whole world has been turned upside down."

Jackson smiled to reassure her as they made their way along the front walk. The old concrete was so cracked and uneven, he almost cupped her elbow to steady her without thinking of the possible negative consequences.

Reaching past her, he opened the worn exterior door and held it while she passed through. He'd seen plenty of dumps before, but this building was close to the worst. Moving out might be the best thing for her. Getting into a safer neighborhood wouldn't hurt, either, particularly since she had her baby's welfare to consider as well as her own.

Jackson paused to knock on the manager's door, then turned to Nicki when no one responded. "Guess they're not home."

"The TV is blasting so maybe they can't hear us over that noise. Let's go on up to my place and see what's left. We can stop by again on our way out."

Jackson's smile spread. "See? There's nothing wrong with your thinking. That's a very sensible suggestion."

"Yup. That's me. All brains."

"Don't put yourself down," he said with a scowl. "I don't know very many people who could cope with the stresses you've faced, and do as well as you are."

Her expression was one of astonishment when she glanced up and murmured, "Thanks."

"No thanks necessary. It's the truth."

"Well, thanks, anyway. It's nice to get a compliment that has nothing to do with my looks—or my cooking."

He was pleased to see her blush slightly, and hear her soft chuckle in spite of the trying situation. The woman was a survivor. That inner strength would stand her in good stead in the coming months, particularly if she failed to find a new job.

Climbing the stairs, Jackson noted that Titan seemed reluctant. That figured. The halls still smelled of smoke and undoubtedly of the chemicals used to formulate the explosive. Plus, the dog would remember this place as being the one that had originally frightened him.

"Let me go to your door first," Jackson said.

Wide-eyed, she stared at him. "You don't think…?"

"No. I don't think there's another bomb. It never hurts to be careful, though. Let Titan and me do what we're trained for. It'll only take a second."

"Okay," Nicki replied, smiling slightly. "But if I see anybody trying to deliver more flowers, I may shove him back down the stairs first and ask questions later."

Jackson could tell she was trying to find humor in spite of her fear so he played along. "You probably won't have to. The department has been grilling every florist in town as if they're hiding Public Enemy Number One behind the bouquets in their coolers. After that, I doubt any of them would accept an order for delivery to this address."

"Good to hear." She rolled her eyes. "Did you figure out where those exploding flowers came from?"

"Not yet. There wasn't much left to go on and

no record of a cash-and-carry sale." He held up his hand like a traffic cop. "Wait there. We'll only be a minute."

He approached the ruined apartment. There was a plain, white envelope bordered in duct tape stuck to the outside of the door.

On the front was printed *#210*. That was all.

Donning latex gloves, he carefully pried the tape loose and opened the envelope, fully expecting another threat.

Instead, he found an eviction notice.

Nicki watched the K-9 officer from afar. She could see that he'd discovered something on her door, but until he motioned her to come closer, she had no idea what it might be.

He handed the paper to her. Immediate incredulity was followed closely by a teary blurring of her vision. She was being thrown out. She'd been a good tenant until recently. Didn't the past count for anything?

"I'm sorry," Jackson said.

What could she say? The notice spelled out several plausible reasons for her eviction, besides the bombing. She sighed and shook her head. "It's okay."

"You were behind in your rent?"

"It's a long story," Nicki told him. "I guess I can understand why this mess might be the last straw. I just wish I still had a job and references so I'd have a better chance of getting another place to live."

"First things first," he said matter-of-factly. "I have permission for you to pick up your clothes and some personal items as long as you confine yourself to the bedroom and bath, in case the crime scene techs want to go over the living room again. Then we'll find you temporary quarters somewhere. Maybe at one of the motels downtown."

"I can't afford to do that," Nicki said, feeling utterly defeated.

"Let me handle the details. The department has an agreement with several businesses to temporarily house crime or disaster victims. Your situation qualifies. Don't worry about the cost."

"Temporarily?"

"One day at a time," he said solemnly.

She had to smile. "How about an hour at a time? I don't think I can handle another day like this one has been. Not all at once."

"She didn't even own a suitcase, so she threw her clothes and stuff into pillowcases. I placed her in the motel closest to downtown, that way she can walk to the store or to church if she wants," Jackson reported to Captain McNeal. "Arnie's delivering her car to her there."

Slade stared into space for a few moments, his blue eyes narrowing, before he replied, "It's stretching the rules to include her in that relief program."

"Yeah…I know. But I couldn't figure what else to do with her. She really seems clueless about her cousin's criminal activities, but she may be in danger just the same. I had her program my private number into her cell phone, too, in case she needs it."

Opening a file folder on his desk, Slade scanned the loose pages. "The Johnson woman is thirty-four. She's hardly naive. She *has* to know more than she's admitting."

"What do you want me to do next? As long as she's out of a job, all we can do is keep an eye on the motel, in case she has visitors, and monitor her calls."

"How's your uncle Harold these days?"

Jackson's eyebrow arched. "He's fine. Why?"

"Just wondering. Last time you mentioned him, he was carping about having to do all the cooking while you were on duty, wasn't he?"

"Oh, hey. Hold your horses, Captain. Harold and I make out fine by ourselves. We don't need a cook. If I was in the market for help I'd hire a cowpuncher to manage my livestock—not that I run many head."

Slade's gaze narrowed. "I've been giving this

situation a lot of thought. I definitely think you need kitchen help. Matter of fact, I know just the person. She's a pro and she needs a job. Plus, if she was at the ranch with Harold all day, he could help us keep an eye on her when you're working. What could be better?"

"Anything but that," Jackson grumbled. "My uncle thinks he missed his calling when he became a sheriff's deputy instead of a stand-up comic. Now that he's retired, he drives me crazy with his stale jokes. Ms. Johnson would never put up with him on a daily basis. I barely manage."

"I'll talk to Harold myself, tell him to cool it and give him the idea that it's an unofficial assignment. He'll love it. Once a cop, always a cop. You know that."

Jackson wasn't convinced that the captain's conclusions were right. He had one last hope. "What if she turns me down?"

"She won't. I've already warned off every restaurant and greasy spoon in and around Sagebrush," Slade said flatly. "Ms. Johnson can't leave this area because she's a person of interest in her cousin's murder case, and she won't find a job in town. She's out of options. She'll agree to work for you."

"You've really thought of everything, haven't you?"

"That's my job," Slade drawled, obviously pleased with himself.

Jackson was anything but happy. "There must be another way."

"Not as perfect as my plan. I think it would be best if you approached Ms. Johnson ASAP. No use taking the chance she might decide to apply for a different kind of position. The sooner she moves out to your ranch and starts cooking for you two starving bachelors, the better."

"And if I refuse to hire her?"

"I can't order you to comply, but you're a good man and a smart cop. If you're truly concerned about her being innocent and in somebody's crosshairs, you'll move her to where she's a lot safer." He paused and closed the file folder. "And if she's as guilty as I think she is, we all need to do everything we can to prove it."

He reached for the phone on his desk and lifted the receiver, holding it while he added, "I'll take care of briefing your uncle. You go hire yourself a cook."

Jackson was muttering to himself all the way to his patrol vehicle. He loaded and secured Titan, then slid behind the wheel. The captain's idea had merit—he simply didn't want to bring Nicolette into his personal life.

And why is that? he asked himself. The honest answer was not only a surprise, it was an unwelcome one. He didn't want to take the chance of getting closer to her. If he had to interact with her all the time, he'd have to really guard his heart because he already liked her far too much for his own good. Or for hers.

FIVE

Nicki had freshened up at the motel and then began using her cell to phone every place she could think of that might need a good cook. After her problematical parting with Lou, she suspected he must have been bad-mouthing her because all her polite inquiries about work were summarily dismissed.

Discouraged, she was planning to make the rounds in person, first thing in the morning, when there was an unexpected knock at her door. Was it safe to answer?

One look through the peephole showed she had nothing to be afraid of this time. The exterior walkway lights illuminated a familiar, most welcome figure.

Grinning broadly, she jerked open the door and greeted the K-9 officer. "Hello! What a surprise." She scanned the sidewalk. "Where's your furry buddy?"

"In the car. Can we talk?"

"Sure. Come on in," she replied.

"You aren't afraid of harming your reputation?"

Nicki had to laugh. "Me? I'm pregnant and alone, just got fired…and my apartment was bombed right before I was evicted. How much worse can my reputation get?"

"You have a point there."

He removed his cap and stepped through the door. The way he was worrying the brim of the hat telegraphed unusual apprehension, particularly since his demeanor was normally so calm and unruffled.

"So, what brings you here, Detective Worth? Am I in trouble again for something I didn't do? Because if that's what you came to tell me, I'd just as soon skip it."

"Actually, no," he said slowly.

"Then what's wrong? You look as if some low-life just tried to kick your dog."

"You're mistaken," Jackson insisted with a smile that seemed forced to her. "Actually, I came to tell you I've arranged for your undamaged furniture to be stored, and found you a new job."

"Really?" Nicki was so elated, she almost forgot herself and hugged him the way Southerners commonly did when celebrating good news. "Where? Did the Sagebrush Diner reconsider?"

"No. Nothing like that. This is a private residence that needs a cook. I figured, since you were so short of cash, you wouldn't care where you worked."

"I guess I don't. What's the catch?"

"No catch. You'll have room and board plus a negotiable salary. You'll be expected to serve three meals a day and keep the kitchen clean. Anything you need will be provided to you, within reason of course, and you'll have your own private room with a bath."

"Go on. Who's my boss? Some lecherous old guy who'll chase me around the kitchen for fun?"

"I hope not." He blushed. "The only older man in the house will be my uncle Harold, and I'll make sure he's on his best behavior."

Nicki could feel the beginnings of a headache thrumming at her temples. "Hold on. You're asking me to work for your uncle?"

"And for me. Harold and I live together on the ranch I told you about. He's been managing the place when I'm gone but he hates to cook and when he tries, it's barely edible." A smile quirked the corners of Jackson's mouth. "Just don't tell him I said so, okay?"

"Slow down. I haven't agreed to take the job. I don't want charity."

The K-9 officer seemed to be warming to his subject because his smile widened more naturally. "Believe me, you'll earn every penny. Harold is a nice guy but his sense of humor can be a bit much sometimes. Your only problem with him will be trying not to groan when he tells the same lame joke for the tenth time."

She met his eyes. "Where will you be all this time?"

"At home, whenever I'm not on duty. I don't have to stay in town as long as I can be paged and respond quickly. The ranch is only about a twenty-minute drive from the station."

"What about housekeeping? I'm a cook, not a window washer."

"No windows." Jackson raised his hand as if taking an oath. "I promise. We have an older woman who comes in to clean once a week. Other than that, it's just Harold and me and Titan. I was hoping that wouldn't be a problem for you."

"I guess it isn't," Nicki said after a short pause. "When do I start?"

"Um, well, I suppose you should spend at least one night here to give us a chance to get a room ready for you."

"Very sensible. One thing, though."

"Yes?" he asked.

"I won't stay at the ranch if I get an offer for a regular restaurant job here in town."

"Fair enough." He squared his hat on his head and touched the brim politely. "Good night, Ms. Johnson."

"Under the circumstances, I think you should

start calling me Nicki," she said as she saw him to the door. "I prefer it."

"All right. I guess you can call me Jackson."

"If I'm working for you, I think it's more proper that I use your job title or your last name," she replied flatly.

"You called Lou by his first name and he was your boss, too. I hope you don't think working for me is going to demean you…Nicki. I'd never do that."

"Okay…you win. Jackson it is," she said with a smile, wishing her cheeks didn't feel so warm all of a sudden.

Standing at the door and watching him climb into the SUV and drive off, she found herself trying to figure out what he was up to. It was nice of him to offer her a job. However, she wasn't quite ready to view his motivation as totally altruistic.

Still, it didn't matter, did it? She'd be working steadily, and if something else came along, she could move back into town. It wasn't as if she had a lot of furniture to put in storage, or anything else to tie her down. And the fresh air of a ranch environment would be good for the baby.

She rested her hand lightly at her waist and said a silent prayer for her unborn child. She'd already seen a doctor and been told that everything was fine, but that didn't keep her from worrying.

Or from remembering what had happened when she'd broken the news to Bobby Lee.

They had been watching an end-of-season football game in her apartment, sharing the sofa that now lay in tatters. Nicki had snuggled up and rested her head on his muscular shoulder. "I have something wonderful to tell you, Bobby Lee."

"Not now, Nicki. The score's tied and they're going into overtime."

Feeling so safe, so filled with joy, she couldn't wait a second longer and blurted, "We're going to have a baby."

The game on TV forgotten, Bobby Lee slowly lifted his booted feet off the coffee table and sat up straighter. He was staring at her as if she had just spoken in a foreign language. His jaw hung slack.

"Isn't that great?" Nicki asked, confused because of his strange expression. "Before we know it, we'll have the big family we talked about."

Instead of smiling and hugging her the way she'd anticipated, however, the tall Texan jumped up and began to yell.

Nicki was flabbergasted. "What's the matter, honey?"

He continued to rant, pace and throw things until his face got so red she wondered if he was going to have a literal fit.

Finally, he returned to lean over her. His volatile mood had caught her by surprise, but that was nothing compared to the intimidating look he flashed her way.

"Thought you'd trap me, huh? Well, you can forget it," he shouted. "I'm too young to settle down."

The feeling of dread that had enveloped Nicki at that time returned in the present. She remembered saying, "But, we love each other. You asked me to marry you."

She shivered, recalling the sarcastic laugh that had bubbled up from the man she'd expected to spend the rest of her life with.

His sneer had been almost as bad. "Of course I said that, darlin'. It's not my fault you bought the fairy tale, lock, stock and barrel. That's why I like to date older women. They're so desperate they'll believe anything. Besides, how do I even know the kid's mine?"

Silent tears were bathing Nicki's cheeks just as they had when Bobby Lee had revealed his true colors. How could she have been so blind, so naive? Thirty-four wasn't that old, was it? Of course not.

But she had been a terrible fool. She had yearned to believe that someone loved her the way Bobby Lee had sworn he did. That had been her downfall.

Disgusted with herself, she dabbed her cheeks

with a tissue. It was a good thing she'd found forgiveness in church and knew that God was merciful because she certainly needed His help starting over.

It did occur to her that perhaps meeting the K-9 cop was a part of the Lord's ultimate plan for her protection. If she hadn't had to nearly get blown up to initiate their encounter, she might have been more likely to assume that divine intervention had been at work.

Thoughtful, Nicki realized she needed to say a prayer of thanks for Jackson's generous job offer. That, she could do. Meaning it from the bottom of her heart was another matter. It wasn't easy to give thanks for a situation that hadn't turned out anywhere near the way she had envisioned.

Her ideas and her prayerful pleas to her heavenly Father had been specific. His answers, however, were far from what she'd expected.

That realization brought a contrite smile. If she truly trusted God as she'd vowed she did, she would manage to thank Him no matter how things turned out.

Nicki closed her eyes, folded her hands and began, "Father, thank You. I don't understand what's going on but I want to, so please help me. I'm doing the best I can. Honest, I am."

It wasn't a polished prayer like the ones she

had heard spoken in church, but it was sincere and straight from her heart.

And, in spite of her misgivings about pretty much everything else these days, she knew God heard her and accepted her just as she was, flaws and all.

That, alone, was enough to bring fresh tears to her eyes and a true spirit of thankfulness to her heart and soul.

Pensive, she walked to the window of the small motel room and looked out, intending to direct her attention heavenward.

The sun had set. Moonlight gave a surreal cast to the dimly lit parking lot, and made the distant hills seem to shimmer—hills she would soon visit when she reported to her new job.

Nicki was actually looking forward to the peacefulness of nights spent on a ranch. There was something special about standing quietly in the twilight and listening to chirps and coos of nocturnal birds and insects. Perhaps there would even be a porch swing where she could sit and let go of her worldly cares more fully.

Lost in thought, she blinked, then tensed. Was that a shadow moving near her parked car? Could someone have followed her? She hadn't thought about hiding her whereabouts by vacating her ruined apartment in secret. Her only focus had been on salvaging her possessions, and getting another roof over her head.

Nicki held very still and peered into the darkness. The harder she stared, the more the images seemed to flicker and waver.

She switched off the bedside lamp to better hide her presence, then quickly returned to her vantage point. There was nothing out there. No bogeymen, no crooks, no stealthy adversaries of any kind.

"It was my imagination," she insisted, speaking aloud to help reassure herself. "I'm tired and stressed, that's all. There's nobody lurking. I'm perfectly safe."

Nevertheless, she double-checked the lock on her door and threw the dead bolt, as well. If they wanted to get to her, they were going to have to break down the door.

"Which is exactly what the police did when Murke came after me," she murmured, pocketing her cell phone. "And it only took them a few seconds to get in."

She glanced at the bed, then at the closet. If she took the quilted spread off the bed, folded it and used it as a mattress on the floor of the small closet, she'd be fairly comfortable. That way, if anyone snuck in, they wouldn't find her easily. And, as long as she stayed fully dressed, she'd be ready to flee at a moment's notice.

"That idea is so foolish, you should be ashamed," she countered, lecturing herself as if she were two separate people. "Either God is watching over you or He's not. Which is it?"

Heaving a sigh, Nicki whipped the comforter off the king-size bed and started to fold it. Since the Lord had given her a keen mind, she figured He expected her to use it. If nothing bad happened during the night, fine. If someone did come after her, they might think she'd moved already and leave right away rather than stay to search the room.

As an afterthought, she stuffed two of the three pillows under the blankets on the bed as if she were actually lying there. Yes, it was silly. And, yes, it demonstrated doubt where she should have been showing trust.

But it wasn't all that far-fetched to think that she might not be totally secure, even here. If somebody intended to harm her, she was not going to make it easy for them.

Tucking the pillowcases filled with her clothing under her head and reclining atop the folded quilt, she pulled one edge of it over her like a blanket, then pushed the sliding closet doors closed. Confined to the tiny area she felt much safer, as if she, like her baby, were enclosed in a cozy womb.

Nicki closed her eyes and began to pray as her mind calmed. In the background, normal noises from other motel guests and passing street traffic faded as weariness finally overtook her.

Jackson figured it would be best to speak with his uncle in person before just showing up with Nicki, so he notified his captain of his plans, then headed northeast toward the ranch.

It wasn't a big spread but it was enough to satisfy his urge to be a part of rural Texas culture. He ran about twenty head of Herefords, give or take a few spring calves, and had enough grazing land that he only had to supplement their feed with baled hay during the winter or during an occasional, long, dry spell.

The house was a simple, one-story rock building with a red tile roof and white wood trim. The older barn was painted to match. Neither he nor his uncle saw a need for fancy landscaping, so the lawn area was basically rocks and desert flora with a smattering of wildflowers in the spring. Other than that, the place tended to look deserted unless there were vehicles parked in the yard.

Tonight was no different. There was one lamp burning in the front room. A single bulb on the porch glowed as Jackson pulled around back.

Harold threw open the door and wasted no breath on pleasantries. "What's all this about a homeless woman coming to live with us? I thought you liked our arrangement. No muss, no fuss."

"I know, I know. It was the captain's idea." Jackson held up his hands, palms forward, in a gesture of surrender as he shouldered past his uncle with Titan at his side. "Don't worry...it shouldn't be for long. We need to keep an eye on her and this was the best place to do that."

"Who says?"

"Like I just told you—it was Captain McNeal's idea."

"You went along with it pretty easy. How come?"

Jackson watched Titan head straight for his full food and water bowls. "I can see a need, that's all. Besides, as McNeal reminded me, you hate to cook."

"I'd rather live on peanut butter and stale crackers than let a stranger mess with my grub. What makes you think this woman can do the job?"

"Anybody can cook better than you and I do," Jackson countered. "Didn't the captain tell you? She used to be a short-order cook at the truck stop out on the highway."

"He never said a word about that," Harold replied. "Just kept goin' on about needin' me to spy on her. What'd she do, anyway?"

"Remember when Rio was dognapped and the captain's father was assaulted, too?"

"Of course. Your team got the guys who kidnapped that Billows kid who witnessed the whole thing, but the police dog is still missing. What's that got to do with this woman we're supposed to watch?"

"We think it's all part of the same overall problem. The rash of murders, the drugs, everything. What we can't figure out is who's killing off all the midlevel criminals in their organization. That's where Nicolette Johnson comes in. Her cousin, Arianna, was part of the gang that's apparently been behind most of the felonies in Sagebrush lately."

"Arianna Munson? Wasn't that case solved?"

"Not entirely. Arianna did kill Andrew Garry, but she also supposedly left behind clues to the crime syndicate's operations. A lot of people, my captain included, think our new cook holds the key to some important code the gang had, whether she realizes it or not."

"What're we supposed to do? Grill her for answers while she grills our dinner?"

Jackson rolled his eyes. "Something like that. Just try to be nice to her, will you? She seems like a pretty decent sort."

"How'd she end up homeless?"

"That was partly my fault. Somebody left a bomb outside her door and I didn't protect her well enough."

The older man eyed the dog licking the last bit of kibble from his bowl. "Titan didn't alert?"

"He did fine. I was too slow. Nicki picked up the explosive device and we just missed getting hurt."

Bushy gray eyebrows arched as Harold began to smile. "So it's *Nicki,* huh? Well, why didn't you say so?"

"Don't look at me like that," Jackson warned. "It's not personal."

"Fine by me. She's probably ugly as a mud fence with stringy hair and missing front teeth. Right?"

He made a face. "Okay, so she's pretty. So what? That doesn't change a thing."

Jackson would have felt a lot more confident that his excuse was credible if Harold had not walked off, chortling to himself, as if somebody had just told a really funny joke.

Truth to tell, Jackson hoped the joke was not going to be on him because thoughts of Nicki were beginning to take up an awful lot of room in his busy mind.

He not only cared about her well-being, he had begun to worry about the health and safety of her unborn child. If that wasn't crazy, he didn't know what was.

SIX

When Nicki awoke the following morning at the motel, she was stiff and sore and sorry she had given in to irrational fear. Nevertheless, she had slept soundly on the floor and was now ready to tackle anything, particularly her new job.

Slowly pushing open the sliding closet door, she got to her feet and stretched. In midyawn, she gazed across the room and gasped. The door she had so carefully locked was standing ajar!

Not only that, sunlight streaming through the doorway revealed that the blankets she had tucked around the bed pillows to replicate her own body had been thrown back, exposing the ruse.

Her wide-eyed stare swept the area in an instant. She was clearly alone, yet her heart continued to pound and her whole body trembled. Her unnamed enemies had been here while she slept. Why they hadn't bothered to check the closet was beyond her. The only reason she could see for her narrow escape was that the Lord must have been watching over her.

Pulling her cell phone out of her jeans pocket as she rushed to slam and bolt the door, she paged through the stored numbers until she came to Jackson's.

One push of a button and it was ringing on his end. He barely managed to say, "Hello," before she blurted, "They're here. They found me. What should I do?"

"What? Who? Slow down. Where are you?"

"In my motel room. The door was open. They pulled back the blankets. They were in here. They had to be!"

"Are you alone now?"

"I—I think so. I was hiding in the closet and…"

"Okay—I'm on my way. Keep the door locked. I'll call the station for you. Don't come out until they send someone over or I get there."

"I'm really scared," she whispered.

"It'll be all right. Just try to stay calm."

She heard his voice fade for a minute as if he might have tucked his phone under his chin so he could pull on his boots. "Can—can you stay on the phone with me?"

"Yeah." He paused momentarily then shouted, "Harold! Call the station and have them send a unit to the Sagebrush Motel, room 12, code 3. There's been a break-in."

Cupping her phone in both hands, Nicki sank to the edge of the rumpled bed. At that moment, her choices were to sit or fall flat on her face, and she figured she'd be in better shape if she acted quickly.

It was only after she was perched on the mattress and starting to calm down that she realized she might have inadvertently damaged important clues.

She sighed regretfully.

"You still there?" Jackson sounded concerned.

"I'm here. Just disgusted with myself. I made another mistake and sat down on the bed. I'm sorry if it messed up evidence."

"Don't worry. Chances are, whoever was in your room was smart enough to wear gloves," he told her.

Nicki huffed. "Is that supposed to make me feel better? Because if it is, it didn't work."

Jackson had nearly reached the motel when he heard sirens in the background of his telephone connection to Nicki. "Sounds like help is arriving. It sure took them long enough."

"I was about to say the same thing," she replied. "Where are you?"

"Passing the truck stop. I'll be there in a couple more minutes."

"Good. I suppose I'd better go outside and tell your buddies that I'm okay."

"Only when you're positive they're actually coming to the motel. Let them get all the way to your door before you open it."

Although she acknowledged his orders, he was far from positive she was going to obey. There was a streak of stubbornness in that woman that was part bravery, part foolishness. In sticky situations, he was never quite sure which element was going to prevail.

He wheeled into the motel parking lot and slid his gray pickup to a stop behind the black-and-white patrol car. His K-9 unit shared the headquarters building with the regular police, but their system was separate so he wasn't that well acquainted with everyone.

Plus, he hadn't taken the time to change into his uniform. He flashed his badge for identification and nodded a terse greeting as he approached. "Morning. Find anything?"

The taller of the two officers shook his head. "Naw. Just a hysterical female. Probably forgot to latch her door and imagined somebody snuck in."

"You didn't turn up anything suspicious? No pry marks on the door?"

"Nope. Not a scratch."

"Okay. I'll take over," Jackson told them dismissively. "Thanks, fellas."

Nicki was standing outside her room door with her arms folded across her chest when he turned. Her hair was mussed and she looked as if she'd slept in her clothes, but he'd never seen her look lovelier. She was also eyeing him.

"About time. You look a lot more like you belong in Texas when you're wearing jeans and that kind of boots."

"I got ready in a hurry," Jackson said with a welcoming smile. "Apparently, you did, too."

"Actually, I never unpacked. I decided to sleep on the floor in the closet last night and it turned out to be a good thing. Whoever broke in didn't spot me."

He cupped her elbow and led her to his pickup truck, shielding her with his body as if expecting imminent attack. "I want to hear the whole story, from the beginning. What possessed you to move into the closet in the first place?"

"Intuition? An answer to prayer? I don't know. Since I've only been a committed Christian for a month or so, I have no past experiences to judge by. Maybe God put the idea in my head."

"How can you be sure you locked up properly? If you were in a hurry, the door might have popped open by itself. The other cops said there was no sign of forced entry."

Her fists rested on her hips and she stood firm, chin jutting. "You sound like them. I know I locked the door because I'm already paranoid, okay? And I put a couple of pillows into the bed so it would look as if I was still there."

"Well…" Jackson could tell she was getting upset with him but felt it was necessary to be certain something truly had gone wrong.

"Well, unless pillows can kick off their own covers, *somebody* else is responsible," she insisted. "Those blankets were thrown aside just like a person would do if they were trying to uncover a sleeping victim. That could have been me!"

"Okay. I'm convinced." He opened the truck door and pointed. "Get in. I'll go get your clothes, tell the manager to leave the room just as it is and schedule a CSU sweep. They probably won't turn up any clues, but as far as I know, they're not too busy to give it a quick once-over."

"Are we going to your ranch?"

"Yes. Sit tight. I'll be right back."

Although Jackson hated to be even a few steps from her, he had parked where he had full view of her room so he could also continue to observe her from there. The mussed bed was as she had described it. So was the closet. He swept up the pillowcases filled with her clothing, checked to make sure there was no one hiding in the bathroom and locked the outside door.

Hurrying back to Nicki, he pushed the cases

across the seat to her and slid behind the wheel. "We'll stop at the office and make sure they understand that your room may be a crime scene, then head for the ranch. That okay with you?"

"I was hoping maybe I could stop and get a few more things from my apartment. We left in such a hurry yesterday I didn't even think to bring a toothbrush."

"Make a list and I'll pick up anything you need. We're not going back to that apartment. At least not this morning."

He wondered if he'd overdone it with the stern tone, so he chanced a sidelong peek. Instead of the angry glare he had expected, however, Nicki appeared to be stifling a smile. "What's so funny?"

"You are. You don't have to bark at me, you know. I'm a reasonable person. All you have to do is state your case plainly and simply. I'll understand."

"And then you'll do exactly as I say?"

This time she did laugh. "I don't know if I'd go quite *that* far."

"Uh-huh. That's what I figured."

"But I will do my best to use the brains God gave me," Nicki assured him. "In spite of everything that's happened lately, I am learning."

"Have you made up your mind which side you want to be on?" he ventured smoothly, wondering if she'd been frightened enough to want to confess her deepest secrets.

When Nicki glared at him and said, "I have always been one of the good guys, whether you believe me or not, Detective," he was sorry he'd been so blunt.

She seemed innocent enough, at least in his eyes, but that was no guarantee she really was. His opinion had already been skewed, and he was getting more and more convinced that Arianna's dying words might not have referred to Nicki.

But if not her, then whom? And what was the code the woman known as the Serpent had hinted at? Most deathbed confessions were taken as authentic, yet it was always possible that Arianna hadn't known how close she was to taking her final breath, and had been lying in the hopes of diverting suspicion.

Jackson made an effort to concentrate on his driving while his mind spun like a Texas tornado. Everybody, his boss included, thought Nicolette Johnson was guilty. So what was his problem?

He took a deep, settling breath and shook his head in disgust. If he were honest with himself, he'd have to admit that he was starting to really like this woman. Not only was she naturally pretty, she had favorably impressed him with her courage and fortitude, not to mention her intelligence.

Positioning herself in the closet instead of occupying the comfortable bed had been a stroke of genius—one that might not have occurred to him even on his best day. He was, however, far more capable of defending himself from criminal attack than she was.

That was one of his biggest concerns. Although Nicki was admittedly smart and brave, she was still a lone woman against forces of evil that had already committed numerous murders in Sagebrush. Jackson did know one thing. Until they tracked down the person or persons in charge of the criminal syndicate and put an end to their reign, *nobody* would be safe. Least of all Nicolette Johnson and her unborn baby.

Nicki chose to avoid further conversation as they sped out of Sagebrush toward her new job. What was the matter with this man? Why couldn't he take her at her word when she was as much in the dark as the police were? Good old Arianna. Leave it to her to cause trouble, even after she was gone.

A twinge of guilt pricked Nicki's conscience. It had occurred to her to pay her estranged cousin a visit and tell her how wonderful it was to be a Christian, but there hadn't been time. Or had there? She supposed she could have made the time if she'd been convinced it was the right thing to do. Then again, if she had gone to see Arianna recently, there would be an even bigger reason to suspect their complicity.

The landscape changed little as they left the outskirts of Sagebrush. If there was one remarkable thing about south Texas it was its consistency. Trees grew well when clumped near settlements, yet struggled to survive along only seasonally wet streambeds.

Since the spring rains had arrived, there were broad fields of wildflowers, particularly delicate bluebonnets, the state flower. They were not always found in such abundance because everything had to be just right for them to sprout. Happily, this had been a banner year.

Jackson slowed to turn off the highway onto a narrow dirt road. "This is it. Take a good look so you won't miss the driveway when you come and go."

"I'm going to be free to do that?" She was astounded.

"You won't be a prisoner, Nicki. I can't force you to stay at the house all the time. But I do recommend you stick close to my uncle, particularly when I'm gone."

She eyed him suspiciously. "Why? Is he my bodyguard?"

"In a manner of speaking...Harold's a retired

former sheriff's deputy. He's usually armed to the teeth."

"What should I expect, a Wild West show?" She gave a nervous laugh. "Am I going to have to wear a sunbonnet, bake biscuits from scratch in a woodstove and draw water from a well?"

"Not hardly."

She could tell from the way Jackson was gripping the truck's steering wheel that he was tense. That sign of emotion took her aback. Here was a guy who faced explosive devices for a living, yet he was nervous about bringing her to his home. What had she gotten herself into? And, come to think of it, how did he expect her to drive away when they'd left her sedan in town at the motel?

"I just had a thought," Nicki said. "How will I get my car?"

"Arnie can tow it again if he has to." Arching a brow, he glanced over at her. "Why? Are you planning a getaway?"

"No. Just trying to get all my ducks in a row. There's a lot to think about. For instance, what about my bedroom suite and the clothes I didn't have time to pack? Or the pots and pans in the kitchen? The fridge came with the apartment, but there was some extra food in there and in the pantry, too."

"The furniture will be stored for you as soon as

possible, and I can have the rest of your personal things boxed up. I hadn't thought about disposing of the food, though."

"No problem. I'll phone Pastor Eaton and have him give it to the needy or take it to the teen center for me. That makes more sense than hauling it all out here. Is that okay with you?"

"Sure. That's real neighborly of you."

"You act surprised. I keep telling you I am not a bad person."

"I never said you were," Jackson replied tersely.

"You mean other than being sure I was in cahoots with my cousin and hiding important clues?"

"Yeah. Something like that." He nodded toward a single-story, rock-faced ranch house. "There it is. What do you think?"

The first words that popped into her head remained unspoken. Words like, *plain* and *sad* and *stark*. What she said was, "It has a lot of wonderful potential. I can imagine climbing roses to match the red tile roof twining around the porch posts. And maybe more bluebonnets with marigolds or something else yellow lining the front walk."

"Um… Sure. I guess… Harold and I aren't gardeners, although he did raise some great-tasting tomatoes last year before the weather got too hot."

"Is that him on the porch?" Nicki asked, pressing her fingertips to her mouth to keep from laughing.

Jackson coughed and stared. "Whoa. It's either Harold or Pancho Villa. I'm not sure which."

Nicki lost the battle to remain serious and giggled. The man was wearing an embroidered, black velvet sombrero and vest. A leather bandolero filled with cartridges was draped across his chest, and he was holding a rifle in both hands as if preparing to take part in an old Western movie.

"You did say he had a sense of humor but I was expecting stale jokes, not a vaquero's costume."

"Harold is one of a kind. Come on…I'll introduce you."

The older man made a deep bow and swept his sombrero off his balding head as Jackson led Nicki up the front porch steps.

"Buenos días, señorita," Harold said, propping the rifle against the railing so he could spread his arms wide. "I am pleased to welcome you to our hacienda. As they say, *'Mi casa, su casa.'"*

"Thank you." Nicki offered to shake hands. "It's my pleasure, Mr. Worth."

"Please, call me Whatsit. Or Matchless, if you prefer." He chortled. "Get it? Matchless Worth?"

"Good thing your real name is Harold instead of Les," Nicki quipped.

The older man slapped his leg and began to

laugh heartily. "Oh, I like this one, son. She's a corker."

When she looked over and saw Jackson rolling his eyes dramatically, she joined in with a soft laugh of her own. So this was the character she'd been warned about. He had already won her over by going to so much trouble to lighten the mood surrounding her arrival.

"I'll bring Nicki's things," Jackson said to his uncle. "You show her to her room."

"By way of the kitchen," Harold said with a wide grin. "I don't know about you two but I haven't had breakfast yet."

"Let her get settled," Jackson warned. "She's had a rough morning already."

Nicki let the older man take her arm and lead her into the living room, where Titan arose from his bed at one end of the sectional sofa and greeted them like long-lost friends.

They paused long enough to give the big Lab a pat before Harold asked, "What kind of a rough morning?"

"I don't know if I'm supposed to talk about it," Nicki was saying just as Jackson joined them.

"Might as well fill him in," the K-9 detective said. "Knowing Harold, he's already heard most of it on his scanner."

"A harmless little vice of mine," Harold admitted. "Never could break myself of wanting to know what all was happening around here. Besides, somebody has to keep an eye on that dog and his partner."

"I imagine you worry a lot when they're on duty," Nicki said. The expression on Jackson's face at that moment was so serious, it caused her to frown. Had her innocent comment about worry touched a nerve?

When the time came that she was finally alone with the older man, she was going to ask about Jackson's background. Even if Harold refused to answer, she'd still know more than she did thus far.

Nicki changed the subject. "Tell you what. Why don't I start by looking over the kitchen, and make a shopping list? That way, when Jackson goes to work he can stop at the grocery store in town and pick up what I'll need."

"I wasn't planning on leaving today," he countered.

His uncle laughed. "Don't be silly. Nicki and I will get along just fine. You go on. And take that chowhound of yours with you before he eats us out of house and home." He turned to Nicki with another wide grin. "The kitchen's through there. I'll go fetch you a pencil and paper."

"I think I've been accepted," she said with relief.

Jackson nodded. "Yeah. Looks like it." He was

scowling and making no effort to hide his un-
pleasant attitude.

"I thought you wanted me here. Why are you
acting as if you don't?" she asked.

"Forget it. It's not important."

If Jackson had been the only one involved, she
might have pressed him for an explanation then
and there. Since he was not, she figured she could
take her time. Harold was no fool, in spite of
his joking demeanor, but he could probably be
counted on to talk too much if she simply asked
the right questions.

One thing she wanted to know was if the police truly suspected her. Another good question
would be, what was bugging Jackson? If he didn't
want her to stay at the ranch, she certainly was
not going to force him to employ her. She'd had
to endure enough feelings of alienation thanks to
Bobby Lee after she'd told him about the baby.
Nobody was going to have that power over her
again. Nobody was going to get the chance to
dump her like yesterday's garbage. If she wasn't
wanted here, she would leave.

Where will you go? she asked herself. *Bobby
Lee isolated you from all of your friends, and if
you simply leave town, the police will think you're
even more guilty.*

Unfortunately, Nicki had more questions than

answers. One thing she did know, however. She was innocent of everything except being too gullible.

And that had led to a sin that would have lifelong consequences.

SEVEN

"You got her settled?" Slade McNeal asked Jackson when he reported for duty later that morning.

"Yeah. Harold's making her feel right at home." He arched a brow. "What's new around here? Did any more lab results come in?"

Slade shook his head solemnly. "Nothing useful. We already knew that ballistics on the bullet that killed Andrew Garry didn't match the ones they dug out of one of the low-level thugs and his buddy a couple of months ago."

"What about the gun Derek Murke used to shoot Lexi?"

"No match there, either. I wish we could pin the murders on him, but if he did shoot those others, he used different pistols." The captain leaned back in his desk chair and laced his fingers behind his head. "I hope you have better results getting info from that cook."

Jackson huffed. "I'll be thankful to get a word or two in edgewise. Harold is really taking his so-called assignment seriously. He's running around armed to the teeth. I wouldn't be surprised to find out he's wearing an ankle holster, too."

"At least he's had the right training to keep from shooting himself in the foot."

"That is my fondest hope," Jackson said with a wry smile. "If there's nothing special you need from me right now, I thought I'd take Titan out to the training yard and polish his skills a little."

"Fine with me. Lee's out there working Kip."

"Good. Thanks."

Jackson was looking forward to talking with his old friend, Lee Calloway. They'd been buddies for so long it seemed as if they had always known each other. However, now that Lee was spending every spare minute courting the amnesia victim who'd finally been identified as Lucy Cullen, they didn't have many chances to just hang out.

Lifelong commitment was starting to look like an epidemic among his peers. First Austin Black fell for Eva Billows while the K-9 teams were searching for her kidnapped son, Brady. Then Lucy and Lee got together, followed by Valerie Salgado and FBI agent Trevor Lewis. There was so much romance in the air, it was getting annoying, particularly since Jackson had made up his mind long ago, after a series of failed romances, that marriage and a law-enforcement career didn't mix.

He pushed open the rear office door, led Titan through the kennel area and exited onto the lawn of the fenced training yard. He ordered Titan into a holding crate so he could set up a test in the field, then hailed his old friend with a wave as he approached.

Kip, Lee's black-and-white border collie, was lying on the grass in the shade, panting and obviously taking a well-deserved break.

"Hey, Lee. How's it going?"

"This dog's better than ever." The sandy-haired, muscular officer shook Jackson's hand. "He should be, considering all the practice he's had finding cadavers lately. I'm almost afraid to take him for a walk around town these days."

"Yeah, I know what you mean. Every time Titan sits down, my heart starts to pound and I expect an explosion—even when he's not supposed to be working."

"At least we got to the Munson woman before she died."

"A lot of good that did. We still haven't figured out what her last words meant."

"You will. The captain tells me you're working to gain her cousin's trust. I should think Ms. Johnson would be delighted to confide in you after you saved her skin."

"Yeah, well, I hired her to cook at the ranch but so far we haven't had time to talk much."

"It's sure pretty out there this time of year," Lee said with a contented sigh. "Lucy and I really enjoyed our picnic out there a while back." He brightened. "I have a great idea. Why don't you host a barbecue get-together for our team and we can all check out your new cook."

"That might not be a bad idea. I'll see what McNeal says. I know it would do his kid a lot of good to be around our dogs more. Caleb really misses Rio since he was taken."

"Yeah, I know. Having Rio's sire, Chief, around is nice, but it isn't the same. Caleb never bonded with him the way he did with Rio. They were kind of raised together."

"True. You through training Kip or do you want me to hide and play dead?"

"You smell too good to make a practical dummy," Lee quipped, slapping him on the shoulder. "I know you're not wearing aftershave to impress me."

"No. Of course not."

"I thought maybe you were sprucing up to impress your new cook."

"Don't be silly. Just because *you're* in love and acting silly doesn't mean it's catching."

Lee's grin widened and his dark eyes gleamed. "Who said anything about *love,* bro?"

The warmth spreading up Jackson's neck and coloring his face was telling. It was also very embarrassing. His mind might be made up about staying single for the rest of his life but obviously his heart wasn't so sure.

Suddenly, the urge to return to the ranch and check on Nicki in person hit him like a sucker punch. He stood stock-still, absorbing the unsettling thought and trying to make sense of it.

Was he crazy?

Or was the Lord trying to tell him something?

He hadn't been a particularly faithful churchgoer, but his belief system was strong.

It had also occurred to him, more than once, that he might have been pushed into her life in order to help her, to protect her from whatever evil forces were lurking in and around Sagebrush. There were plenty to choose from. He sure wished he could put names and faces to their deeds, and make sure those who were responsible were locked up.

Leaving Lee and Kip and heading back toward the kennels for privacy, Jackson pulled out his cell phone and dialed the ranch. Nicki probably wouldn't pick up the house phone, but Harold was there.

At least he was supposed to be. Nobody answered.

After counting ten rings, Jackson hung up and tried Nicki's cell—with similar negative results. The hairs at the nape of his neck prickled in warning. His intuition had been right—something had gone wrong.

He unfastened the latch on Titan's kennel box door and ran back into the office with the faithful dog at his heels. Passing the day secretary, Lorna Danfield, he shouted, "I'm headed for my ranch. Taking the SUV. Page me if you need me."

The middle-aged, blonde woman merely waved as if it was normal to see someone racing out the door.

Jackson was thankful that nobody had tried to stop or question him because he wouldn't have lingered to talk.

Harold should have answered the house phone even if Nicki chose to ignore her cell, Jackson reasoned. His jaw clenched. If anything bad had happened to either of them, he was never going to forgive himself.

Nicki had shared coffee and toast with Harold while making a list of necessities for the ranch kitchen. "I'm not a fancy chef and don't pretend to be," she told him. "I hope that's going to be okay with you and your nephew."

"Fix lots of meat and potatoes, and you'll get no complaints from us," he said with a smile. "The freezer's full but I never know what to do with anything except put burgers or steak on the barbecue."

"I think I can manage a little variety and still keep my job," Nicki murmured. "Shall we go to the store?"

His bushy gray brows knit and he shook his head. "Best not leave, at least not 'til Jackson gets home, or he'll have a cow."

"All the more livestock for this ranch," she gibed. "Is that where the rest of these cattle came from?"

"Funny." Harold chuckled. "Actually, we bought most of 'em at an auction up in Odessa. The bull's purebred Hereford but the cows are crosses. Gives 'em hybrid vigor."

"So I've heard."

"Are you into ranching?"

"No. I used to date a cowboy." Sobering, she folded her arms across her torso.

"I take it he wasn't a keeper. Did he hurt you bad?"

"Bad enough," Nicki admitted. There was a sweetness behind the older man's question, and kindness in his gray eyes. "I may as well tell you since it's going to be obvious soon enough. I'm pregnant."

"I kinda figured it was something like that."

"You did?"

"Yeah. I've never seen my nephew so protective of anything, man nor beast, before. He may not know it but he's got a soft spot for helpless things."

Nicki's jaw dropped. She was about to insist she was far from helpless when she realized he could have meant her unborn child. In that case, there was no reason to take offense. "The baby, you mean?"

"'Course. I've seen him risk his life in weather that would've kept any sensible man inside, just to go lookin' for one lost calf."

"I don't know my Bible very well, but that sounds like something Pastor Eaton preached about recently."

"One lost sheep, you mean? I guess that could represent all of us. You a believer, Nicki?"

"Yes. I hit bottom after Bobby Lee dumped me, and the only way to go was up. When I turned my life over to Jesus, I thought things would get better, though."

"Maybe they have and you just haven't seen the outcome yet," Harold offered. "Tell you what. Why don't we leave the kitchen chores for now and take a tour of this spread? Jackson and I are pretty proud of the way we've fixed up the place."

"I'd love to see it all." She patted the cell phone in her pocket to reassure herself it was still there before she smiled and said, "Let's go."

The flatbed ranch truck was sitting next to the barn where he'd last seen it. Harold's private mini-pickup sat nearby and Nicki's car was out front by the covered porch, right where the tow truck had dropped it.

When Jackson arrived, he stopped in the portion of the yard farthest from the buildings. Leaving Titan behind for the present, he stepped out and drew his sidearm. He didn't want to call undue attention to himself in case there was trouble. He also didn't intend to get caught unprepared.

His boots crunched lightly on gravel as he crept closer, and peeked in the windows at the north side of the main house. There were no signs of a struggle. There was also no one visible.

Jackson kept his gun pointed to the sky as he proceeded around to the rear. Loose chickens were scratching and pecking the ground. They didn't seem upset, but that didn't mean a whole lot since hens were far from intelligent.

Still, he mused, they might be acting flighty if there was trouble brewing.

Pausing to listen carefully, Jackson thought he heard voices in the vicinity of the barn. He was certain of it by the time he'd reached the outside of the front sliding door.

That was Nicki. Laughing. And Harold was chuckling along with her.

Furious, Jackson burst in on them.

His uncle's initial reaction was to make a grab for his own sidearm before he realized who had just popped through the door. A moment later, he started to grin. "Whew! You sure know how to make an entrance, son. Put that gun away. We're fine."

Jackson holstered his weapon but not his temper. "Where *were* you?"

"Right here. Just like I promised we'd be. Who put the burr under your saddle?"

Instead of answering, Jackson glared at Nicki. "Where's your cell phone?"

"In my pocket."

"You might try answering it when it rings."

"It didn't. Ring, I mean." She pulled it out and held it in her palm. "I've had it with me the whole time. See?"

He grabbed it, flipped it open and checked. "How long has it been since you charged this thing?"

"I don't know. Is the battery low?"

"*Low* is not the word for it. It's dead."

"Then that's why I didn't answer it," she said nonchalantly. "It never rang."

Jackson felt as if he were a deflating balloon. These two were acting as if he was overreacting while he was barely able to keep from shouting at them for their carelessness.

"No harm done," Harold said brightly. "As you can see, we're just fine."

"Well, I'm not," Jackson countered. "You scared

me out of my mind. When neither of you answered your phones, I thought..."

Nicki laid a hand gently on his forearm, her touch warm through his sleeve. "I'm sorry. We both are. But since you're here, would it be possible to make a grocery run?"

"How can you even think about shopping?"

"Somebody had better," she countered. "If you expect me to prepare a week's worth of food without running back and forth to town, I'll need a properly stocked kitchen."

"Fine. Fine," Jackson grumbled. He knew he sounded peeved but that was just too bad. His heart was racing, even now, and perspiration dotted his brow. If he hadn't been so thankful that he could barely think straight, he knew he'd still be shouting.

"Harold and I will take my car, then," Nicki said. "That way I won't be alone coming home with the groceries, and you can go straight back to work. You do need to do that, don't you?"

"Yeah, sure."

What he wanted to do was grab her by the shoulders, stare her down and make her understand how desperately worried he'd been. The possible tragic scenarios that had filled his mind as he'd raced to the ranch had seemed so real, he'd been sure one of them would come true.

Yet there stood Nicki, smiling sweetly, and behaving as if he were the one with the problem.

I am, Jackson realized with a start. Something about this pretty young woman had brought out the gladiator in him...and he didn't know what to do about it. Only one thing was certain at this point. If he didn't keep a lid on his feelings, he was not only going to be less effective at his bomb-detecting job, he was going to lose his objectivity.

Turning away, he gritted his teeth. He had ceased being impartial with regard to Nicolette Johnson the moment he had met her. And things were only getting worse.

"If we swing by my old apartment on the way home, I can run in and get the charger for my phone," she told Harold and Jackson as they loaded sacks of food into the trunk of her old blue sedan.

When neither man commented, she added, "It'll only take me a second."

Jackson frowned. "Tell me where it is and I'll go up and get it."

"Wish I could. I think it's in a kitchen drawer but I'm not positive." She smiled. "Besides, I want to pick up the potted plants outside on the fire escape, too. They'll add some color to your front porch. It certainly needs it."

"You had this in mind all along, didn't you?"

"Actually, no. I thought of it when I saw the geraniums for sale in the store's nursery department. I did intend to ask about the charger, though. You're the one who was complaining that my phone was dead, and since it's different than yours I'll need to have my own charger."

"All right." Muttering under his breath, he slid into the SUV and slammed the door while Harold and Nicki got into the other car.

"Is he usually this grumpy?" she asked as she started the engine and backed out.

"Nope. I don't know what's gotten into him. He's usually pretty mellow, especially since he's been back in the States."

"He told me he and Titan worked together in the military," Nicki said. "I got the idea it was pretty rough on both of them."

"Yeah. It was." Harold heaved a deep sigh. "And there was the other, too."

"Other?"

"Uh-oh. Shouldn't have said that."

"Maybe not. But since you have, you may as well go on with the story. I'll find out eventually, anyway, and it might help me keep from making Jackson any madder."

"That's debatable." He cleared his throat and shook his head. "There was a girl. She'd promised to wait for him, and I guess she sort of did, until she found out he was planning to become a cop when he got out of the service. Then she hit the road and married a banker. Said she wanted a safe, normal life." He snorted wryly. "Whatever that is."

"That's too bad."

"Yes, and no. She wasn't right for him in the first place. Too prissy and self-centered. Worst of all, she didn't like having animals in the house. Not even Titan."

Nicki chuckled. "That bad, huh? Well, Jackson's life certainly hasn't been dull, particularly recently. What do you know about all these killings?"

"Like your cousin's, you mean?"

"My estranged cousin. The newspaper says Arianna's death is tied to at least two or three others, maybe more. The problem is, Jackson thinks I know something secret, and I don't have a clue what he's talking about."

"Then just bide your time," Harold advised. "My nephew can be stubborn, but he's fair. He'll see the truth eventually."

"I wish I knew what the truth was. It's really hard to stay out of trouble when you have no earthly idea who the bad guys are or what they're after."

"We'll keep you safe," he promised.

Nicki glanced in her mirror and saw the K-9

vehicle following. She believed both men were sincere. She also knew that they were nearly as blind to the dangers as she was.

Someone was lurking out there in the beautiful Texas countryside, ready to jeopardize her happiness, and perhaps end her life the way they had ended others. The person or persons didn't have a face she could identify or a plausible reason why they wanted to harm her. They simply did. And as far as Nicki was concerned, she was as helpless as a newborn kitten—blind and floundering, looking for comfort and security that were being withheld.

At that moment, just as she was telling herself she had never felt more alone or abandoned, she realized she was far from it. There was a fatherly figure seated beside her. A knight in shining armor was driving behind. And a sweet dog that was just about the smartest canine she had ever met was also along for the ride.

That was her personal army. The individuals the Lord must have sent. How could she question their sincerity or their skills when they were undoubtedly the answers to her most fervent prayers?

EIGHT

Jackson saw Nicki pull into the driveway to the apartment building and stop halfway. He parked behind her.

"I'll be right back. Stay," he told Titan.

As expected, the dog lay down on the seat and acted as if he understood. For all Jackson knew, he did. There were times when his furry partner seemed to almost read his mind.

"I wonder what he thinks of my overblown interest in this woman?" Jackson muttered to himself. The unspoken answer brought a smile and a shake of his head. It was a good thing Titan couldn't express his opinion or he'd probably tell his master he was acting like a fool.

"What if they've changed the locks?" Nicki asked, leaving Harold to wait in the car with the groceries, and falling into step beside Jackson.

"Then we'll get the manager to open up for us. I doubt they've done anything yet, though.

We made arrangements to pick up your bedroom suite for storage so there has to be access."

"Are the crime scene people finally through?" she asked.

"Yes. The lab was happy with their samples."

"So, what was the bomb made of?"

He arched an eyebrow at her and cocked his head. "Why do you ask?"

"Curiosity. Is it some big secret?"

"We prefer to keep most details of active cases confidential. I will say I was surprised, though. The explosive wasn't very powerful."

Nicki huffed. "Oh? Tell that to my TV. As a matter of fact, tell it to my landlord."

"You don't need to worry about this place anymore," Jackson said as he led the way up the stairs and tried the door, surprised to find it unlocked.

He held out an arm to block her way. "Hold on. Let me check it out first."

"Do we need to get Titan?"

"I doubt it. You don't live here anymore, so there should be no reason for it to be booby-trapped."

"Oh, that's a comforting thought. Thanks for mentioning it. I feel so much better now."

He could tell from her wry tone that she was being facetious, but nevertheless took his time. Finally, convinced that the apartment was safe, he motioned for her to enter.

"Where do you think you left the phone charger?" he asked.

"In a kitchen drawer or cupboard, most likely. I usually plug it in over the counter." Nicki pointed to the remains of the sliding glass door that led to her tiny porch and fire escape. "The geraniums I want are out there. Do you mind getting them for me? I don't want to spend any more time here than I absolutely have to."

"Sure. No problem."

As Jackson picked his way cautiously through the shattered glass and rubble, his footsteps crunched as if he were walking on gravel. The drape that had once covered the door was frayed and smoke-tinged, and fluttered in the slight breeze.

He pushed the fabric aside and stepped out, shading his eyes against the glare from the setting sun. Below him lay the back fence of the apartment grounds and beyond that the Lost Woods, a largely undeveloped area of Sagebrush with a wild history of its own. Between legends from the past and current crime statistics, plenty had occurred in those woods over the years.

Jackson was bending to pick up the two small flowerpots Nicki wanted when something in the distance caught his eye. He froze, crouching behind the wooden railing, and blinked to see if he was imagining things. He wasn't.

A tall figure, clad in black, was walking slowly along a path. His body moved like that of a male, and he not only wore a hat that shaded his face, it looked as if he might also be wearing a ski mask.

That anomaly was what originally caught Jackson's attention. Unless the guy was up to no good, there would be little reason to hide his features. Besides, although April weather could be nippy once the sun set, this particular day had been balmy.

From inside the apartment, he heard Nicki announce, "Found it!" and then heard her footsteps approaching.

Remaining crouched, Jackson held up his hand, palm out. His "Shush" was little more than a loud hiss.

To his relief, she froze where she stood, and waited. "What is it? What's wrong?"

"Down there," Jackson whispered. "In the woods."

She tiptoed closer and cautiously peeked around the edge of the opening. "What? All I see is a dog."

"A *dog?*" He scrambled to where she was standing and straightened so he'd have the same vantage point. She was right! Not only was the figure working a dog on a long lead, the animal resembled a German shepherd. Could it be Rio?

He flipped open his cell and pushed speed dial

for the station rather than use his radio, and take the chance of the transmission being overheard. If that really was Rio, and the man with him was part of the crime syndicate they'd been after, they might have more men as well as sophisticated eavesdropping equipment positioned nearby.

"This is Worth, K-9 unit 463," he said, turning away and cupping his hands around the phone. "I'm at the apartment on Lost Woods Road, second floor rear, where we had the bombing. I can see a masked individual in the woods behind this building and there's a shepherd with him. It might be Rio. I can't be sure from so far away."

Turning, he peered out once again. "Yes, I can still see them. They're moving slowly, headed southeast. Looks like they're alone, but the trees have leafed out so I can only catch a glimpse when they pass through a clearing."

He paused to wait for orders, and his gaze met Nicki's. She was good and scared, yet safe enough as long as she stayed away from the window, and didn't try to follow him if he was sent to apprehend the suspect.

"What are you going to do?" she whispered.

Jackson pressed the phone to his ear and nodded, listening, before he said, "Copy. We'll stand by."

"We?"

It was more a squeak than a word. If the situation hadn't been so serious, Jackson might have laughed. "I meant Harold and I," he explained. "They want me to observe and wait for backup. There's a chance that isn't Rio but in case it is, we want to be able to track him—and the man—to see what they're up to."

"Won't he get away?"

"Not from the dogs on my team," Jackson assured her. "Austin Black's bloodhound, Justice, is one of the best trackers in the state. And with the help of our narcotics and protection dogs, plus Titan, we can cover all the bases. We'll get him…I hope."

"You had me convinced until you added that at the end." Nicki made a face. "I had no idea police work entailed so much waiting."

"It doesn't always." He forced a smile for her benefit. "Patience is a virtue, you know."

"Yeah, well…"

The wry look she was giving him brought sincerity to his grin. "I know. It's one of the hardest things for me, too. I want results ASAP. I suppose most folks do."

"What do we do now?"

"I wait here and watch. You go down and tell Harold what's going on, then stay with him until the patrol units get here."

Jackson could tell she wasn't eager to follow his orders, probably because she didn't want to be alone long enough to return to her car. Unfortunately, the only other option was to keep her with him and if he did that, Harold might panic and cause a ruckus when he saw the black-and-whites arriving.

"If you're too scared, I guess you can wait up here," he finally said.

"I'm not scared. Not one bit. I just don't want to miss any of the excitement." She shivered. "I don't like it up here, though. Too many bad memories."

Jackson assumed she was referring to the bombing, although he supposed it was also possible that she was upset because she had shared that apartment with her no-good ex-boyfriend. The notion of Nicki in another man's embrace tied Jackson's gut in a knot the size of Amarillo.

"Just go, then," he said brusquely, handing her the small potted plants. "I'll hold down the fort. Harold needs to be briefed, and since he hates to carry a cell phone, somebody will have to deliver the message in person. Are you up for it?"

"Sure. I'm good." Clutching the pots, she started for the door, then hesitated. "You're sure it's safe for me to leave?"

"If I didn't think so, I wouldn't send you," he said. "I'm only seconds away on one end of your errand, and Harold is the same on the other end. We're both armed. Believe me, it's not a big risk."

"Okay, okay. You don't have to sound so impatient. I'm going." She juggled her plants to display the small phone charger before shoving it into a pocket. "I got everything I came for."

As soon as Nicki passed from sight, Jackson was sorry he'd sent her down alone. Yes, he believed it was safe. And, yes, he knew he and Harold would be plenty of protection. Yet there remained a niggling sense of worry that he could not shake.

In the woods below, the man and dog were passing beneath a canopy of trees, and out of his line of sight. If they continued in the direction they'd been headed, it might be several more minutes before he could actually see them again. That was long enough for him to run to the door and watch Nicki make her way downstairs.

Taking one last look at the area he'd been observing so closely, Jackson sprinted across the small living room, hit the hallway at a run and caught a quick glimpse of Nicki's back.

"Make it okay?" he called after her.

She paused and turned to wave at him. "Fine. I can see Harold."

Jackson flushed, embarrassed. Of course she was okay. It was silly to think that anyone would bother her when she was accompanied by two strong men. *Armed* men. His well-marked vehicle was parked right behind her car, and anybody who had been in Sagebrush for very long knew that Harold, being a retired deputy, was prepared for just about anything, too.

Nicki was with his uncle now, Jackson reassured himself, so she was perfectly safe. He knew that with every ounce of his being. Yet his heart was still racing and his breathing more ragged than it should have been.

He quickly returned to his vantage point above the Lost Woods. Vegetation was thick and lush this time of year due to the spring rains. Even later, when the grass dried and most of the wildflowers were gone, the trees would retain their leaves. Texas cottonwoods and other indigenous varieties of foliage were tough. As tough as the folks who had tamed this country a century or more ago.

A woman like Nicki would have fit right in with those brave settlers, Jackson mused. She was resilient. Courageous. Willing to do whatever she had to in order to survive.

His breath caught. Was she so determined to succeed on her own that she'd withhold evidence of a crime? Many people in her position might. Despite his instincts about her true virtue was it possible that Nicki was playing him for a fool?

In his heart lay a firm *no.* His fertile mind,

however, continued to doubt. Soon, everyone should know the truth. The trouble was, he was already so biased in her favor he wondered if he was going to be able to accept anything except complete innocence.

Turning his attention back to the woods, he forced himself to concentrate on the job at hand. Nobody would be safe until they put an end to the current crime wave. It was possible that the key to solving at least some of the puzzles, perhaps all of them, was right now lurking beneath those trees.

"Where are you?" Jackson whispered into the wind. "Where did you go? Come on, come on. Step into another clearing so I can see you again."

What could that man be searching for? he wondered. And if that truly was Rio, why go to the trouble of stealing him when there had to be other elite, multipurpose canines available.

For an instant, it occurred to Jackson that the theft of that particular police dog might have been a direct attack on Captain McNeal. He dismissed the notion of a vendetta as being too far-fetched. There had to be other possibilities.

They had already tied the deaths of some middle-management criminals like Frist, Garry and even Munson to a powerful criminal organization. The conundrum was why someone involved with them felt it was necessary to kill his or her own men—or why Arianna Munson had apparently murdered Andrew Garry, leading to her own death at the hands of FBI agent Trevor Lewis.

"So, Arianna, what did you mean when you tried to warn your cousin with your last breath?"

Jackson suppressed a shudder. Clueless or not, Nicki was still in trouble. Deep trouble. He pictured her standing in a dry desert streambed while a sudden storm dropped tons of rain in the distant mountains, and a wall of water began to rush toward her. That was the kind of desperate situation she was trapped in. And he had no idea how to rescue her before a destructive wave of wickedness swept her away like a flash flood.

Nicki climbed into the car with Harold and locked the doors.

"What's up? You look a fright. Where's Jackson?"

"Upstairs. He spotted somebody in the Lost Woods and called for backup. I'm supposed to tell you to stay here and wait."

She could tell from the way the older man had tensed and begun to fidget that he was not pleased to have to stand by when something exciting was unfolding. Truth to tell, Nicki wanted to go back to be with Jackson, too.

"We could leave Titan to guard the car and go back," she suggested. "Together, I mean."

Harold's bushy eyebrows knit. "You ready for that?"

"Sure. Why not?" The way his eyes swept over her as if making an assessment gave her pause, but she insisted, "I'm not scared. Honest."

"It's not a matter of courage," he explained. "It's a matter of duty. Jackson and I are committed to taking care of you, and if that means sitting here and twiddling my thumbs while we wait for more backup, then that's what I'll do."

Nicki's decision was made in an instant. Giving in to impulse she jumped out and leaned down to speak through the open door. "Have it your way. I'm going back upstairs, so if you really want to watch me, you'd better get a move on."

Behind her she could hear the older man muttering under his breath. He was coming all right—huffing and puffing and talking to himself with such intensity, she had to smile. Like his nephew, Harold Worth was the kind of man she could count on in any circumstance, no matter what. That was not only comforting, it buoyed her overall spirits a great deal.

When she reached the top of the stairs, she waited for him to catch up before pointing. "It's down there. End of the hall. Jackson is at the back window looking down into the Lost Woods."

"Lead on," Harold said with a scowl.

Nicki gave him a sweet smile. "You wanted to come up here and you know it, you old faker. I just gave you a good reason to do it."

"Never said I didn't." He fell into line next to her, sighing and shaking his head. "What I didn't want to do was expose you to any more possible danger."

"From who?" Nicki asked. "The bad guy is down in the woods. He has no idea we're watching him."

"He may not but that doesn't mean he's alone. If you're going to play detective, you'll need to learn to think outside the box. See threats behind every door. Assume the worst of everybody until you prove otherwise."

"Is that how you see me?" she asked, lowering her voice now that they were approaching the open apartment door. In her heart of hearts, she hoped he was going to reassure her that he knew she was innocent because that would mean that Jackson probably felt the same.

"I think you're a smart woman who's too naive for her own good, among other things. I also think you've got more guts than half the men I know."

"Thanks, I guess."

"You're welcome." He paused and held out his arm to block her path, reminding her of the way Jackson had also behaved. Without looking at her, he said, "Shush. Slowly now," before he eased through the doorway.

Nicki followed. She was glad she was behind Harold when Jackson spun around and glared at them.

"Didn't you tell him to wait?" the K-9 officer demanded.

"She did," Harold answered for her. "I thought three pairs of eyes would be better than one, that's all. Can you still see him?"

"No." Jackson shook his head. "I lost him over that way, about ten o'clock."

Nicki understood he was referring to the position of the numbers on a clock face and peered in that direction. "I don't see a thing except trees."

"Me, either," Harold added. "How long ago did you lose sight of him?"

"Just a couple of minutes."

"There's nothing over that way except forest, is there?" Nicki asked.

"I seem to remember an old chapel and a graveyard," Harold said thoughtfully. He looked to his nephew. "Am I right?"

"I think so. Keep looking."

Nicki could tell from Jackson's expression that he was formulating a plan. She stepped aside to give him room to pass as he reentered the apartment and made another call.

"This is Worth, K-9 unit 463 again," he began.

As Nicki listened, he gave the dispatcher the information Harold had provided and suggested a dual approach to the woods.

"That's right. Nobody uses the chapel anymore, but there are still new burials in the cemetery from time to time. I don't have the GPS coordinates. Tell the units to take Lost Woods Road clear to the end, past the park, then make a right on the dirt road and keep going. The old church is sitting in a grove of trees and the graveyard is behind it."

Nicki didn't look away when Jackson's gaze met hers. She knew he was upset with her, yet she also thought she sensed his grudging respect. Although it was beyond her fondest dreams that he might actually want her with him, she chose to believe that he had at least come to terms with having her there, probably because Harold had accompanied her.

That was okay with her. Almost anything was, as long as she was included as if she belonged.

No, she countered. *That wasn't entirely true.* She had standards, principles, a newly enforced sense of right and wrong. From the moment she had truly become a Christian, she had understood that. She had not been a bad person before, she was simply a better one now.

A flash of light in the distant forest jarred her from her reverie. She shaded her eyes with one hand and tapped Jackson's shoulder with the other, then pointed.

"Look. Over there! I just saw it for a second. It looked like a reflection of something shiny."

"From what? Could you tell?" He bent over her, almost placing his cheek against hers to get the same perspective.

Nicki caught her breath, astounded by how acutely his nearness was affecting her. "I—I think it might have been from a mirror or something. It's really hard to tell with the sun so low. I suppose I could have imagined it."

"Could it have been reflecting from the chrome or windshield of a car?"

"I suppose so." She strained to listen, to hear other sounds, in spite of her pounding pulse. "Do you hear a motor?"

"I'm not sure. Stay here with Harold."

Jackson left her and raced for the door.

Nicki heard his boots thudding down the stairs. She turned to the older man. "Where is he going?"

"Best guess? I'd say he's headed out there to chase whatever you saw," he said with a shrug. "Uh-oh."

"What?"

"Over there, where you thought you saw the flash of light. There's a cloud of dust. See? It looks pinkish in the twilight."

"Yes! The man with the dog is getting away, isn't he?"

Harold huffed and his shoulders sagged. "Sure looks like it to me."

Closing her eyes, Nicki prayed, *Please, please, please, let Jackson be in time,* then added, *and keep him safe.*

She knew, without actually forming the words, that she wanted to say, *Because he is so very special to me.*

Before she had time to take another breath, she realized that, whether she said so out loud or not, the Lord knew exactly what truths were hidden in her heart.

In the space of a mere couple of days, she had formed a ridiculous attachment to the handsome Texas cop.

She might be wiser than before because of what Bobby Lee had done, but apparently her heart hadn't learned a thing.

NINE

Jackson had radioed his position as he drove into the woods on unmarked dirt roads. Chances had been slim from the outset that he'd arrive in time to overtake whoever had been working that German shepherd, but he'd had to try.

By the time his team had gathered at the place where he'd last spotted the shadowy figure, man and canine had disappeared. So had the sun.

"Titan won't be much use to us in this case," McNeal said, muttering unintelligibly and sounding more than disappointed. "Why don't you head back to the apartment and see if Harold has anything to report?"

"Yes, sir."

Returning to his car, Jackson dialed Nicki, wondering if she'd had the foresight to plug in her phone and let the apartment electricity power it. To his astonishment, she had.

"Hello?"

"I don't believe it! You charged your phone."

"Actually…I can't take credit for that. It was your uncle's idea. Where are you?"

"In the Lost Woods, moving west. Searchers are spreading out from my original sighting, but it looks like the guy got away. I'm going to check out the area where you saw the flash before I come in, just in case."

"Why don't you turn on your red lights? That will help us see you and maybe tell if you're close."

"Will do." He reached down. "There. Can you see that?"

"Yes. It looks as if you're a little west of the place. Harold and I both saw dust rising over there after you left us."

"How much farther is it?"

There was a short pause before she answered, "Harold says maybe half to a quarter of a mile. He thinks it was near that old church he mentioned."

"Okay. I'll relay your information and keep going. The team is using the bloodhound. They won't disturb him while he's tracking, but I can have a look right now."

"I wish I could be there, too. Any chance Harold and I could come? We'd stay out of the way. Honest."

"You two need to go home and put the groceries away," Jackson said, knowing what her reaction would be.

Nevertheless, it made him smile when she said, "Phooey. There's nothing perishable and you know it."

"Well, it was worth a try. Let me talk to my uncle."

In an instant, Harold was clamoring for more information.

"Simmer down," Jackson said calmly. "There's nothing either of you can do here except mess up the few clues we do have."

"Like what?" the older man demanded.

"A few fresh footprints and some tire tracks from my original observation. Not a whole lot, I'm afraid."

"What about the old church?"

"I'm almost there but I'm going to stage and wait—unless I see somebody. Austin is working Justice. I don't want to get ahead of that team in case they end up coming this way."

"Fine. We'll take the food back to the ranch, pick up the ranch truck and meet you near the abandoned chapel. Should take us about an hour." He exhaled sharply. "That ought to be long enough for the bloodhound to get his sniffing done."

"No! I don't want you to bring that woman into this." Jackson knew there was too much emotion in his tone, but he couldn't help himself.

He heard his uncle chortle. "*Me* bring *her?* It's

more like the other way around. I practically had to hog-tie her to keep her up here after you ran off."

In the background, Nicki was loudly insisting otherwise.

"Okay, okay. I'll meet you in the woods in an hour," Jackson said. "You won't have a reliable phone until Nicki's is fully charged, but you can use the two-way radio in the truck. Meet me where the road forks just before you get to the turnoff for the chapel. Understand?"

What Jackson really wanted was a firm commitment from the retired deputy and was satisfied when Harold said, "Agreed. We'll wait for you. Just don't keep us cooling our heels for too long." He paused to chuckle. "I don't know whether I'm ever going to be able to convince our new cook that she belongs back in the kitchen instead of on a stakeout."

The resulting racket in the background, compliments of Nicki, made Jackson smile as he ended the connection. As long as she was with Harold, he wasn't too worried about her. The way he saw it, she'd probably be safer in his uncle's company than she would be at the ranch by herself.

"And, we still need to keep a close eye on her, just like Captain McNeal said," he muttered.

Could Nicki really be withholding evidence?

Everything about her pointed to innocence, yet she was clearly a clever, determined person.

She's also a new Christian, he reminded himself. That wasn't proof of her truthfulness by itself, but it did tend to support her claims. The question was twofold; had she reformed enough for it to make a difference, and had she needed to do so in the first place? Yes, she had made a big mistake by getting pregnant, but that didn't make her a bad person any more than any other sin did. It simply made her human, something they all were whether they happened to be believers or not.

Speaking of being human... Jackson mused. Against regulations he was losing his personal battle to keep from caring too much for a suspect, and there didn't seem to be a thing he could do to stop himself.

Nicolette Johnson had gotten under his skin. Big-time.

Nicki grew more and more enthused as she and Harold drove toward the Lost Woods. He had insisted that they grab a quick bite while storing the groceries at the ranch house, and for that she was thankful. Her easily upset stomach seemed much happier when it wasn't empty.

"I have to admit," she began, "I feel a lot better since I ate. I had no idea that would help."

"Always did wonders for my wife," the older man said.

"You had a family?"

"Yes." His smile was wistful. "Still do. My two kids moved to Florida with my ex and her second husband. Now that they're grown they call or email pretty regularly so it's not so bad."

"Is that how you and Jackson got together?"

"Because we were both alone, you mean?" He smiled to soften the question. "Not exactly. I'd been living in Texas for years before he joined up and was sent overseas. When he asked me to look after his ranch for him, it was a perfect arrangement for us both. After he got home, he invited me to stay on. There's no place I'd rather live so I agreed. I love to explore this country."

"Is that how you learned about the abandoned chapel?"

"Matter of fact, it is. I saw a line of cars headed into the Lost Woods one day and decided to see where they were going. Turns out there was a funeral in the old church graveyard. Apparently, some families have large plots and mausoleums there and keep using them."

"Makes sense. My cousin, Arianna, was buried in Dallas because that's where her parents' graves were. My folks' graves are there, too."

"Sorry for your loss. It's hard being the last one left, isn't it?"

Nicki nodded thoughtfully before she replied, "Yes. I was hit with that realization after I heard that Arianna was gone—although I do have a half sister somewhere back East. I know it's silly, but I feel kind of like an orphan."

She didn't flinch when he reached over and patted her hand where it rested on the seat between them. His knuckles were enlarged and his skin calloused, yet his touch was gentle. "You'll never be alone as long as you're a member of God's family. And if you ever want to add an old uncle like me, I'm available for adoption."

"Thanks," Nicki said. "I'll keep that in mind. It's been so long since I felt as if I was part of a real family that I don't know how well I'd fit into one."

"You'll do just fine wherever the Lord sends you," he said with a smile that crinkled the leathery skin at the corners of his brown eyes, and somehow reminded her of Jackson.

That reaction shouldn't surprise me, Nicki reasoned. Pretty much everything, from police work to cowboy boots and Stetsons, reminded her of that man.

Worse, she could hardly wait until they met him at the planned rendezvous. The mere thought of seeing his face, standing near him, watching him smile, made her giddy with joy. It wasn't the same kind of emotional tie she'd thought she'd shared with Bobby Lee. It was more. Much more.

Mutual? Maybe. Maybe not. She and Jackson hardly knew each other, and time would tell. She was already in plenty of trouble without falling for one of the cops who was investigating Arianna's murder.

Nicki crossed her arms and stared through the truck windshield, realizing how foolish she was being to even dream of such a thing. No man was going to want her now. Not when she was carrying someone else's baby. The chances she might have had for a normal life with a loving husband and children had disappeared when Bobby Lee Crawford had tricked her, used her and deserted her. It was over.

Still, it was not her unborn child's fault that she'd made such a terrible mistake. The baby was as innocent of purposeful wrongdoing as she was.

A sidelong peek at the man behind the wheel of the pickup truck showed his concentration focused primarily on the road ahead. However, he also kept glancing in the side mirrors.

Nicki frowned. "What is it? What's wrong?"

"Probably nothing. Sit still. Don't turn around."

She started to do exactly that and had to stop herself. "Why? What do you see?"

"It's possible we've picked up a tail."

"You mean *I* have, don't you?"

Harold's bushy brows arched. "Okay. You have. Now do you see why I insisted you and I stick together no matter what?"

She huffed, "I guess so. I know Jackson wants you to watch me closely because he thinks I'm holding out on him. Hiding evidence. I wish I were. Believe me, if I knew anything that would get all these idiots out of my life and off my trail, I'd be delighted to reveal it."

"You're sure you don't have even a clue? Anything at all? Did your cousin mail you anything or leave any messages? Think."

"No!" she nearly shouted it. "I am exactly what you see, nothing more, nothing less. I'm a short-order cook with no home, a stack of bills that keep piling up and a bun in the oven that turned my life upside down. All I want is some peace and quiet."

After a short pause Harold said, "I believe you. Pull your seat belt tighter and hang on. I'm about to try to ditch this tail."

He made a snap turn south off the highway and onto a bumpy dirt trail. The truck's engine roared and its heavy-duty springs made the tires bounce like overinflated beach balls.

Nicki's right hand grabbed the handhold mounted above the passenger door while her left clamped the edge of the seat.

"You okay?" Harold shouted.

"As good as can be expected. Have we lost him yet?"

"No. He's still back there," Harold yelled. "Grab the radio and warn Jackson."

"What shall I tell him?" She let go of the seat and fisted the mic at the end of a spiral cord.

"That we're being pursued by a black sedan with tinted windows and those new, bright headlights. If this guy is still with us when we get to the meeting place, there won't be any question of mistaken identity."

"Gotcha. What's Jackson's call sign?

"K-9 unit 463. It's his number, four, plus the vehicle ID."

Nicki triggered the radio and broadcast, "K-9 463, this is your ranch truck. We're approaching the planned rendezvous and we have company. Advise."

"How soon?" Jackson replied.

She looked to her companion. "Five to ten," he said.

"Five to ten minutes," she repeated. "The way Harold's driving it may be even sooner."

"Copy. Keep coming. Don't stop where we had planned. I'll be waiting for him."

Nicki lowered the mic. "He said…"

"I heard him. This may get a little dicey. Hang on."

"As if I'm not already," she shouted over the

roar of the engine and the squeaking of the truck as it bounced and twisted over the rough roadway.

Her eyes were wide and she was apprehensive, so filled with adrenaline she could hardly breathe, barely think. How did cops do this without making mistakes or overreacting? Most of the police work she had watched so far had been tedious and rather boring. Being involved in a car chase, however, changed everything. Demonstrated the seriousness of their plight.

And, knowing that Jackson was waiting to leap in to assist them made the situation even more nerve-racking.

For Titan's safety, Jackson had moved him to his crate in the rear of the SUV. Its motor was idling smoothly, headlights off, and the windows were rolled down so he could hear approaching vehicles. The ranch truck was a diesel with a distinctive sound. Mixed with that noise was the higher-pitched whine of a second car.

Jackson's fists tightened on the wheel. "Thank you, Lord, that Harold's driving." If Nicki had been behind the wheel, there was no telling how well she'd have followed his instructions. Probably poorly, judging by past performance.

The light gray ranch truck, referred to in casual conversation as a "dually," had dual sets of rear wheels on each side of the bed and wider fenders to facilitate pulling a stock trailer. Therefore, the truck took up most of the width of the dirt road as it passed, assuring that whoever was following wouldn't be able to easily pass to cut it off.

Jackson was parked where thick brambles hid his patrol car. He let Harold and Nicki fly past his location, then gunned the engine and pulled across the road to block the other vehicle.

A black, compact automobile showed up mere seconds later, its headlights temporarily blinding.

Jackson braced for impact.

The other driver hit the brakes, sending that car into a skid that almost failed to end in time to avoid a collision. Then, all was quiet.

Jackson jumped out, gun drawn, faced the car over the hood of his SUV and shouted, "Police! Hands where I can see 'em. Now."

At first there was no other movement. Then, the car started to back up rapidly. Jackson would have loved to play Wild West show cowboy and shoot out the tires, but unfortunately it was against department policy to use excessive force unless a criminal threatened bodily harm. If the car had kept coming at him he wouldn't have hesitated to fire.

He thought he heard the diesel sound of the ranch truck in the background. It wasn't fading away as he'd hoped. Apparently, Harold's tail wasn't the only one moving in reverse.

Jackson grabbed his radio to alert other units to the problem, then straightened and waited for Harold and Nicki. They arrived so quickly he was positive they hadn't traveled far after passing him.

He holstered his gun and greeted them. "You could have kept going."

"And miss all this," his uncle said with a grin as he stepped down. "I haven't enjoyed myself so much for ages. Did you get a license number?"

"No, it was too dark. But I did radio a description. Units on the highway may still apprehend them." He looked past Harold and saw Nicki getting out of the truck so he called, "You okay?"

"Fine." To Jackson's astonishment she seemed almost as unruffled about participating in the car chase as Harold did and there was an unnatural brightness to her eyes. That was probably not a good sign. Not good at all.

"Okay. Get back in the truck and let's keep going. I told the others we'd check the graveyard. Austin's bloodhound was hot on a trail that led the other way so that's the direction everybody else headed."

"Okay," Harold said with a smile. "Nice drivin', son."

"You're not so bad yourself, old man." Jackson clapped him on the back. "I see you didn't forget the lessons you learned in the police academy."

"There's nothing like a good dose of adrenaline to bring it all back. You want Nicki to ride shotgun with you the rest of the way?"

"Why?" The self-satisfied gleam in Harold's eyes had caught Jackson off guard, but he quickly figured things out and ended the older man's matchmaking efforts. "You two have apparently been doing just fine. Since your tail is long gone and the excitement is over, I see no reason to change the seating arrangements."

"Have it your way." Harold shrugged thin shoulders beneath his Western shirt. "Probably better that way. She didn't seem to mind getting thrown all over the cab of the truck before, so a little more bouncing around probably won't hurt her."

Jackson was not amused. "That's not funny."

"Want to reconsider then?"

"You guys might want to ask my opinion," Nicki interjected. "I do like sitting up high in that truck, but I'd rather have Titan for company." She looked over at Harold and managed a smile. "No offense."

"None taken." He was peering into the rear seat of the patrol car. "I don't see him."

"He's in his crate," Jackson explained. "I suppose I could let him out—as long as you two promise to behave. No more reckless car chases?"

She spread her hands wide, palms up. "Hey, it wasn't our fault."

"Sometimes I wonder…about both of you," Jackson drawled. "Okay. I'll get Titan and put him up front with us. Then let's get this show on the road. I still want to check the old cemetery. You two can come along so I can keep an eye on you."

"It's not too dark?" Nicki asked.

"That's what flashlights are for." He was leading his bomb-sniffing partner around the SUV as he answered. The dog suddenly balked. Stopped. Jackson knew better than to overlook his canine partner's instincts. "What is it, boy? What's wrong?"

The ebony-coated dog was standing motionless, staring into the forest. Jackson tried to follow the same line of sight with no luck.

"What does he see?" Nicki asked.

"More likely he smells or senses something," Jackson said. "Go ahead and get in the car."

"But…"

"I said—" He was about to reinforce his order when the sharp crack of a shot echoed off the surrounding hills. He didn't have to see the precise point of impact to assume it had hit somewhere close by.

"Get down!" he shouted.

Nicki had been holding the side door open for Titan. She dove inside at the same time the dog did, and they ended up sharing a seat.

Slamming the door and throwing himself behind the wheel, Jackson saw Harold doing the same in the truck. They were at a terrible disadvantage since they didn't know where their enemies were or how many they were facing. The only sensible course of action was to flee.

The dually threw up a rooster tail of dust and gravel.

Jackson whipped in behind it. There was a good chance he'd get a pitted windshield out of following this close, but at the moment he could envision a lot worse consequences as a result of dropping back.

"Hang on!" he yelled at Nicki, taking a quick glance in the mirror to check on her.

Her blue eyes were wide, her cheeks flushed, and she was gripping Titan so fiercely, he wondered why the dog was not trying to wiggle loose.

"Another hundred yards or so and we'll be in the clear," he promised.

"Who's shooting? Are they aiming at us?"

"I don't know, and I don't intend to hang around to find out."

The target probably was Nicki, he concluded, although there were unfortunately plenty of folks who didn't care for cops, either. It was remotely possible they had inadvertently encroached on a moonshine still or a drug operation that was hidden in the forest. It was also possible that the pursuers in the black car had doubled back.

Either way, Jackson was thankful that whoever was shooting had such lousy aim.

"Did we lose them?" Nicki called from the backseat.

Jackson was about to tell her he thought so when a rifle shot clapped. The bullet whined. Zinged.

Both rear side windows of the racing SUV exploded, raining down in tiny bits the same way the glass door at Nicki's apartment had as a result of the explosion.

She shrieked, long and loud.

For an instant, he feared the bullet might have found her, too, and his heart almost pounded out of his chest.

"Nicki!"

TEN

Hugging Titan and huddled with him on the backseat, Nicki wasn't sure what had just happened. She knew there had been a shot. And the SUV had been hit. Beyond that, she was clueless.

The first thing she did was take stock of herself. Nothing hurt, nor was she bleeding, so that was good. Titan seemed okay, too, and was trying to lick her face.

That left Jackson. He was still driving through the woods like a madman but that didn't mean he was unscathed. "Are you hit?" she yelled.

"No. You?"

"We're fine. How about Harold?"

"Still going ninety," Jackson shouted. "Stay down, just in case."

Did he think she was nuts? He must, if he felt the necessity to tell her to duck in the middle of an ambush!

Dropping to the floor on her knees, she pulled the quaking dog closer and held him tightly. *Poor guy.* This terrified reaction must be due to his PTSD. Considering how scared she was right now when she'd had no prior experience being shot at, the poor Lab must be frightened nearly out of his mind.

"Titan is shaking really bad," Nicki called from her position on the floor. "What should I do?"

"Just stay down with him. We're almost there."

"Then what?"

She was positive she heard Jackson make a derisive sound before he answered, "We take cover."

That made sense. At least in theory, she reasoned. Since there was supposed to be a chapel at the cemetery, they might find shelter there. As far as she was concerned, particularly lately, church was the perfect sanctuary.

No place is a good place to die, she countered silently. She knew she'd go to heaven eventually. She simply wasn't ready to depart anytime soon. A new life lay ahead of her and her unborn child. She was not about to give it up without a fight.

Jackson had forgotten there were aboveground burial crypts on the cemetery grounds, as well as the tiny rural chapel. The sun had set behind the tree-topped ridge to the west, giving the horizon an ethereal glow. If it hadn't been for the dust the ranch truck had kicked up, he might have missed locating Harold parking his truck behind a mausoleum.

The small building's stone sides were covered with dead vines, and its once pristine walls had turned a dingy white. There was a carved name over the door, presumably that of one of the main families present at the founding of Sagebrush. All Jackson could read in passing was a capital *A* at the beginning of the inscription.

He chose to pass the place where his uncle had stopped, and park behind the chapel while he radioed his position to the station.

"Out. Both of you," he ordered when he was done talking to dispatch. "Keep Titan on the leash and hunker down between this car and the building. That'll give you better shelter."

"Where will you be?" Nicki asked.

He was amazed at the calm strength of her words, the way she seemed able to adjust to any circumstance and roll with the punches, so to speak.

"As soon as I'm sure we're safe, I'm going to go get Harold and we'll check the area. I'd wait for more backup, but it's going to be pitch-dark soon. If we don't find tire tracks or footprints right away, we may as well give it up for the night."

Although it had occurred to him that their choice to drive all the way onto the grounds might have obliterated any latent clues, he still intended to have a look around.

"At least the dark will help us hide from whoever was shooting," Nicki said quietly.

"It will also help them hide from us," he countered. His gun was drawn, every muscle in his body taut as he paused beside her and scanned the otherwise peaceful grounds. "Are you sure you're okay?"

He heard her sigh before she said, "Sure. I have Titan, and he has me. What more could we want?"

"He's not a protection or attack dog," Jackson warned, "so don't expect him to defend you."

"That's okay. I'll defend him if I need to."

"With what? Are you armed?"

"Of course not. I just meant…" She paused and sighed again. "I don't know what I meant."

"Do you know how to handle a gun?"

"Not unless it's the kind that squirts water."

He almost laughed. "Okay. Tell you what. If you want to learn, I'll give you shooting lessons while you're out at the ranch. With real bullets."

"I could never purposely hurt anyone."

"I wouldn't expect you to go hunting down the bad guys, Nicki. I just want you to be able to defend yourself, and know how to react properly if you find yourself in danger."

"Well, in that case, I'm willing." She was stroking Titan's head and scratching behind his ears as she spoke.

"Good for you." Jackson started to straighten and move away. "Now stay here." A small smile resulted when he realized how he could ensure her compliance. "I'm counting on you to take good care of Titan. Understand?"

A nod was all the answer he got. It was enough. Nicki was the kind of person who took every job seriously. She would look after the dog, and by doing so would also be safeguarding herself.

He eased out from behind the parked SUV, his pistol in one hand, flashlight in the other. He'd have to circle the chapel in order to signal Harold. That wouldn't be difficult.

The hardest part of all this was forcing himself to leave Nicki. If he followed his true instincts he'd turn back, put his arms around her…and stay that way forever.

That wasn't smart. Nor was it likely. But it sure sounded like a good idea.

Listening intently, Nicki heard Jackson's footfalls even after he was no longer in sight. He'd circled the building slowly, then started to jog.

She also heard Harold's call to him and his reply. If they felt it was safe to shout at each other, there was likely no further danger. Nevertheless, she chose to obey orders and stay put with Titan.

As time passed, the black Lab calmed considerably, although he continued to pant as if he'd just run a marathon. No wonder, considering how scared he'd been.

Truth to tell, the dog wasn't the only one fatigued after their ordeal. Starting to yawn, she eased down beside him and propped her elbows on her bent knees.

"Well, old boy, what would you like to do now? Huh? How about a game of tic-tac-toe? Oh, you don't play? Too bad. I'm very good at it."

The silliness of the one-sided conversation relaxed her. She slid her fingertips through the dog's short, silky hair and wiggled them all the way down his spine, bringing a happy wag of his tail. "You like that, huh? Good."

Time seemed to drag by. The dim glow of the sun beyond the horizon disappeared completely. Nicki was beginning to get concerned. She shivered. How long should it take to canvas a small cemetery like this? Why weren't Jackson and Harold back by now? Could something have happened to them?

Straining to listen, she heard nothing but the onset of nighttime insect chirps and the calls of a few nocturnal birds. No human spoke. No footsteps echoed through the otherwise silent forest surrounding them. No motors purred or raced, not even in the distance.

Loudest of all was the thrumming of her pulse in her ears, and the rapid breathing of the dog lying beside her.

Suddenly, Titan held very still, closed his mouth and stopped panting.

Nicki tensed with him. She leaned closer, trying to see what he was seeing.

It was impossible. The woods were too dark, too filled with unidentifiable shapes barely defined by the waning moon.

Wind pushed at supple tree branches, making their shadows dance among the headstones and claw at the aboveground crypts like ferocious beasts with long, grasping talons.

She chanced a soft, "Jackson? Harold?"

No one answered.

Her imagination began to create a vivid and terrifying scenario—one in which she was left all alone in the cemetery and villains of every order were closing in on her. On them.

Brushing off the notions as she brushed off her jeans, Nicki stood. The leash was fisted in one hand, the dog obediently poised at her side.

Now what? She had vowed to wait for Jackson's return, yet an awful lot of time had passed—enough to bring the full force of night and cause her to squint, straining to see more clearly. Surely, he hadn't meant for her to stay put this long.

Besides, if his dog was concerned, she should also be.

Still standing outside, she eased open the side doors of the patrol vehicle, looking for some sort of weapon, preferably a simple one. There was nothing except a shotgun, and she wasn't going to take the chance of mishandling it.

The storage area behind the backseat, however, provided an L-shaped jack handle. It wasn't too heavy to carry, yet it would certainly be better than being empty-handed.

It was then that she fully realized she intended to go looking for the missing men. Yes, she had promised to take care of the dog but since he was the one who seemed concerned, it made perfect sense to move.

Titan would lead her.

She would protect him.

The plan wasn't foolproof, it was simply the best choice under these circumstances. At least that was what she kept telling herself.

"Come on, Titan." Nicki took a step forward and he kept pace. "That's right, boy. Let's go see what's been bothering you."

To her astonishment, the black Lab seemed to understand—because he not only started off in a straight line, he began to move faster and faster.

Still clutching the metal jack handle, Nicki had to jog to keep up. The leash was shorter than ones she'd seen before, giving her less leeway to maneuver among the headstones and around trees and bushes.

She'd tripped several times before she gave a hard tug on the line and said, "Easy, boy. Slow down."

Titan turned his brown eyes up at her as if he knew what she wanted. His anxiety, however, was still barely contained.

Nicki gave him some slack. That was a mistake.

The dog lunged forward.

She felt the webbing of the short leash slipping through her fingers. It burned as it chafed her skin.

Titan was loose! Running away.

"No!" Nicki shouted, stunned that the usually tractable animal had suddenly bolted. "Titan!"

Glimpses of his orange reflective collar were visible for a few seconds, but the rest of him blended into the darkness far too well.

Nicki set off in pursuit. If he changed direction, she'd never find him. All she could hope was that his beeline toward his unidentified goal would continue.

She heard his bark fading in the distance as he ran. "Titan!"

Where was Jackson? Where was Harold? *Dear God, help me,* her heart cried out.

Something caught here eye. Was that the dog's reflective collar again? *Praise the Lord. It was.*

Hurrying ahead, she kept her eyes on the place where she'd last seen the bright orange plastic, and thrcaded a path between upright headstones, showing respect by trying to avoid stepping on the ones that lay flat to the ground.

Rounding a crypt, she stumbled. Felt herself falling.

Self-preservation insisted that she drop her makeshift weapon and use both hands to break her fall.

She landed in the loose dirt on all fours. Something large and hard was pressing against her chest, and the fall had knocked the breath from her lungs. All she could imagine was that she had tripped over the trunk of a fallen tree.

Blinking, she pushed away. Levered herself higher. Saw Titan's nose and wide, pink tongue mere inches from her face.

Nicki's relief at having caught up to the naughty dog was short-lived. There was enough pale light from the moon to show her more than she wanted to see.

The tree trunk had facial features! Wispy blond hair. Sunken eyes. Lips that were little more than a gash across the ashen face.

Nicki gasped.

Screamed.

Threw herself backward and gawked in disbelief for a heartbeat, then screamed again. And again.

There, beside her on the ground, lying as still as death, as cold as ice, was a body.

The dog had led her to a dead man.

Jackson was back at his police vehicle, arguing with Harold about where to start searching for Nicki and Titan, when a high-pitched screech split the darkness. "That's her. It has to be. Stay here by the radio."

He drew his gun and started toward the sound at a run, using his flashlight to choose a safe path. If it hadn't been for a multicar accident on the main highway, they would have had plenty of backup by now. Unfortunately, a hunch about trouble in an old cemetery wasn't enough to warrant a full-blown response when there were specific needs that must take precedence. Jackson knew that was department policy, but he didn't have to like it.

"Nicki! Where are you?" he shouted.

"Over here."

He swung the light beam. Nicki was crouched near the ground with the dog standing over her. All the usable air left Jackson's lungs. He was about to shout for Harold when she waved and clambered to her feet.

He slowed only slightly. Holding his pistol pointed at the sky, he clicked off the flashlight and spread his arms as she ran into his embrace. At this moment, he didn't care what protocols they might be violating. He wanted her as close to him as she apparently wanted to be.

"What happened?" His voice was raw with emotion. "Why didn't you stay put?"

"Titan…Titan wanted to come over here. I guess he sensed something was wrong."

"And you listened to a dog instead of me?" In spite of chastising her, he held tight with his free arm.

"I was afraid for you," she said. Her cheek was against his chest and he could feel her trembling. "I didn't know where you had gone…and I thought maybe Titan was trying to tell me you needed help." She took a shuddering breath. "I'm sorry."

Closing his eyes, Jackson sent up a silent prayer of thanks and just held her. She had gone against his orders for his sake. How could he fault her for caring? He probably would have taken a cue from the dog, too, given similar circumstances.

"Just tell me you're not hurt," he said tenderly.

"I'm not hurt." Nicki leaned away slightly and inclined her head toward the place where she'd fallen. "But the guy over there's not doing so well."

Jackson turned and used his flashlight to illuminate what he first thought would be a grisly scene.

Instead, he saw the body of a young man, probably a teenager, in quiet repose. The boy's clothes were starting to deteriorate—particularly at the cuffs and collar—and his shoes were coming apart, but his body was otherwise pristine.

Playing the beam over the emotionless face, Jackson noted unusual puckering and sallow skin tones.

"This isn't a new murder," he announced, holstering his sidearm. "He looks embalmed."

"That explains the open grave."

"Where?"

She pointed. "Over there. I almost fell into it."

Before he could change his mind, he placed a conciliatory kiss on the top of her head, then took her hand. "Your new friend isn't going anywhere. Come on. We'll go back to the car and call this in."

"What do you think is going on?"

"I don't have a clue," Jackson admitted ruefully. "If I was going to rob a grave, I sure wouldn't choose a recent one—I'd go for one of the crypts where the rich folks are interred."

"Who was this man?"

"I'm not positive. I don't want to go any closer and disturb evidence." He felt Nicki's grip tighten, and she lagged back so he paused to ask, "What's the matter?"

"My handprints will be in the dirt next to him.

When I fell I landed right…" She shuddered and swallowed hard. "It was awful."

"I'll run you by the emergency room on our way back to the ranch, so you can get checked out if you want. I hope you don't believe those old wives' tales about expectant mothers getting scared and hurting their babies."

"Of course not."

"Then don't worry, okay? I'll explain everything to the crime scene techs when I talk to them."

"I'm getting pretty tired of being their guinea pig." She sighed. "I know I'm innocent and just wish they'd believe me."

He wished he could ease her mind. He really did. The trouble was, as far as the police were concerned, Nicolette Johnson was in this mess all the way up to her pretty neck.

It was a lot like being stuck in quicksand. The more she struggled and protested, the deeper she ended up sinking. And he was right there with her.

ELEVEN

"His name was Daniel Jones," Slade McNeal told the assembled officers when they'd had a chance to examine the scene at the cemetery. "I went to his funeral about five years ago."

Jackson had his arm around Nicki's shoulders, much to her relief, and gave her a squeeze of support before asking, "How did he die?"

She could tell that the captain was strongly affected but didn't fully understand why, until he explained further.

"Daniel was resisting arrest for dealing drugs. One minute I had the drop on the kid, trying to reason with him, and the next, he was waving a gun at me. I put one bullet into his thigh to stop him. A sniper finished him off before I even had a chance to cuff him."

"I remember reading about that case," Nicki said softly. She looked up at Jackson. "It must have happened while you were overseas. The newspapers had a field day with the story. They kept insisting it was police brutality and that the victim was just a poor, defenseless kid." She shivered, seeing the similarities to her own life when she added, "His mother was raising him by herself."

"That's right," Slade said. "And it gets worse. Daniel's mom, Sierra, was Detective Melody Zachary's sister. Sierra killed herself when she got the news her son had died." He raked his fingers through his short hair. "All in all, it was a horrible mess."

"The same Melody who's the director of the Sagebrush Youth Center?" Nicki asked. "I didn't know that about her. It makes sense, though. I suppose she feels she's helping other kids, like her nephew, to stay clean."

"Yeah." The captain turned and addressed Jackson. "Since your patrol unit is damaged, use your ranch truck to take everybody home. We can handle this. I'll come out to your spread tomorrow to question everyone again."

Slade's frown deepened. "I'll have a few more questions for you, too, Worth. You know the drill. Please refrain from discussing this evening's events with each other or with any outside parties."

"Yes, sir."

Nicki waited until Jackson had walked her back

to his truck before she asked, "Are you under suspicion, too?"

"It's just procedure."

"He looked awfully serious," she remarked.

"That's understandable, considering his prior encounters with the Jones kid. Until tonight, I had no idea the captain was so deeply involved." He paused and glanced back to where floodlights illuminated the crime scene. "I wonder…"

"What?"

"Nothing. We're not supposed to discuss this case, remember?"

She glanced up at him. "Were you planning to talk about what happened tonight?"

"No." Jackson was slowly, thoughtfully, shaking his head. "I was just wondering how a teenager with no money ended up in that section of the cemetery."

"What do you mean? What's so special about it?"

"It's probably nothing. I'll tell you later, after I've had a chance to check a few details."

Harold overheard their conversation. "Tell her what?"

"The choice of grave sites puzzles me, that's all," Jackson said.

"You mean why is a poor kid buried in the Frears section? That's easy. Lots of folks who can't afford their own place end up in there. I imagine, because Captain McNeal and Dante Frears are old friends and former military buddies, there was an arrangement made.

"I was already retired when the Jones shooting took place, but I heard plenty of gossip about it. McNeal was really torn up after it happened. He blamed himself."

"Why? He didn't shoot to kill."

"No, he didn't." Harold was shaking his head. "Just the same, there was some rumor after your captain's wife, Angie, was killed, that maybe somebody was aiming to get back at Slade for the Jones boy's death and blew up Mrs. McNeal by mistake. I guess nobody ever proved a connection."

"Where was Daniel when he was shot?" Jackson asked.

"Come to think of it, right here in these woods. If I was superstitious, I might wonder if there was a jinx on this place."

Nicki didn't believe in such things, but that didn't keep the suggestion of lingering evil from giving her the willies. There was something awfully creepy about running around in the forest after dark, even if she didn't count tripping over an embalmed corpse.

The mere memory of that encounter made her flesh crawl. She had touched him, actually touched him. And although she knew that the young man's soul was long gone from that empty shell, she was nevertheless repulsed.

I should pray for him, Nicki told herself before wondering what good that would do. It was the living, the struggling, the ones still breathing, who needed to be held up in prayer—like the youth center lady named Melody, and Captain McNeal, who kept beating himself up for failing to save a teen who was headed down the wrong path.

And I'll pray for Jackson, she added, feeling her cheeks warm suddenly as she climbed into the truck and scooted to the center to make room for the two men on either side of her, while Titan rode on the narrow seat behind them. She had a good idea what to ask God on the K-9 officer's behalf, and she was going to add him to her prayer list. After all, everybody could use divine help from time to time.

"Like tonight, when whoever was shooting at us missed," she muttered to herself. In the midst of the turmoil, she had failed to give thanks for their survival. Now she made up for that oversight.

They could have all died. It was that simple.

Jackson had assumed his new employee would take a day or two off to acclimate herself, particularly after the harrowing cemetery incident.

He was wrong. He awoke to the smell of fresh-brewed coffee and the aroma of sizzling bacon. If Nicki's cooking tasted half as good as it smelled, he was going to be sure to thank Slade for pushing him to hire her.

Harold was already in the sunny kitchen when Jackson entered with Titan at his heels. "Boy, that smells good."

"I wasn't sure what you preferred so I fixed a couple of different things," Nicki said. "How do you want your eggs?"

"Over hard. Are those waffles?"

Her grin was broad, her eyes sparkling. "Yes. The waffle iron in the cupboard looked so new, I wasn't sure if you'd ever used it."

"I don't know that we have," Jackson admitted as he helped himself to a mug of steaming coffee. "Harold and I never fuss. Anybody can fry an egg. The fancy stuff we get when we eat in town."

"Well, I'm taking orders for supper," Nicki said. "There's plenty of meat to choose from in the freezer. What sounds good?"

"Surprise us. We'll love it."

Titan plopped down at Nicki's feet and looked up at her as if she were the most wonderful person he'd ever met.

She laughed. "I think your dog likes me."

"No offense, but he loves anybody who fries

bacon. You can give him a little taste if you want, just keep it small. He's on a strictly managed diet."

"Yeah, me, too," Harold chimed in, presenting his empty plate. "And I'm the one who's in charge. Two eggs over easy, all the bacon you can spare and a waffle, please."

"Coming right up." She turned back to the stove. "So, what are we doing today?"

Jackson and Harold both said, *"We?"* as if they had rehearsed speaking in unison.

"Maybe I should rephrase that." Nicki was chuckling quietly. "What am I supposed to do while you two go about your business today? I don't suppose you intend to take me back into town, considering what happened the last couple of times I went."

"Not if I can help it," Jackson replied. He sobered and waited until she was looking directly at him before he continued. "I can't order you to stay here. You're not under house arrest or anything. But if you're smart—and I know you are— you'll lay low for a while. Whoever sent you that bomb and made those other threats could easily have been the same ones who shot at us out by the cemetery."

"Really? I thought that was probably because they didn't want us to discover they'd dug up a body." She gave the frying pan a flip and the eggs landed upside down, perfectly centered.

"I don't think so," Jackson said. He accepted the filled plate she passed him. "Thanks."

Nicki wasn't satisfied. "Then what's going on?"

"Know what *I* think?" Harold piped up. "I think it's all cut from the same cloth, so to speak. The killings, the drugs, the bomb, everything."

"Okay," Jackson said as he started to eat. "How?"

"If I knew that, I'd go to work as a police consultant and make a pile of money," the older man said. "I can't put my finger on the reason, but I keep thinking that the crime syndicate has to be at the bottom of everything."

"That doesn't explain why anybody would dig up Daniel Jones's body. He died five years ago and the rash of killings didn't start until recently." Jackson hesitated. "You know, technically, we're not supposed to discuss the Jones case."

"Horse feathers. If we can't separate one from the other, tough. Maybe the connection is the narcotics."

Thoughtful, Nicki leaned back against the kitchen counter and took a sip of coffee. "Suppose Harold is right. Is there a link between those old drug busts and the people you suspect may be responsible for the latest crimes? I mean, why would a successful syndicate all of a sudden start killing it's own people? That's crazy."

"A power struggle, maybe," Jackson ventured. "I don't know. Nobody does."

"What about my cousin, Arianna? What exactly is she supposed to have done?"

Her question made him raise an eyebrow. "For starters, she not only killed Garry, the Realtor, she was involved in the drug business up to her eyeballs. You must have realized she didn't make all her money running that little restaurant."

"How would I know *that?*"

Nicki's defensiveness was predictable. Nevertheless, he pressed on. "Because you'd known her all your life? In order to live such a lavish lifestyle, she had to have had another source of income."

"I never thought about it," Nicki admitted. "I tried to have as little to do with my cousin as possible. She was—she was..."

"Go on."

Nicki shook her head and averted her gaze. "No. I'm not going to say it. It's bad enough that I'm thinking such awful things about her when she's not here to defend herself. Even when we were kids, Arianna had a mean streak. She was always looking for ways to get me to take the blame for something bad that she'd done."

"Is that what you think she was doing when she mentioned a secret code?"

"If she hadn't added *cousin,* I might have my

doubts, but since she did, yes, I do think she was trying to get me into trouble. It wouldn't be the first time."

"Fair enough."

"If it was *really* fair, everybody would believe me when I say I have no idea what she meant about a code or danger."

"The danger part seems to be taking care of itself," Jackson said wryly. "First Murke breaks into your apartment, next somebody sends you a bomb, then we get shot at in the woods. Seems pretty consistent."

"Just what I wanted to hear." Nicki pulled a face. "Not only are there murderous thugs after me, they're reliable, too. How special."

Jackson had to laugh. He finished his meal, wiped his mouth with a paper napkin and carried his plate to the sink.

"I'll do the cleanup," Nicki insisted.

"Sorry. Force of habit. The dishwasher works fine so you shouldn't have too much work to do. After that, the morning is all yours." He turned to her. "Harold will show you which horses are safe to ride and where we keep the tack. Just don't go too far from the house unless one of us is with you."

"Horses won't be a problem," Nicki said, blushing. "I never learned to ride in the first place, and I don't think it's smart to try to learn now."

"After the baby comes, then," he said, noting that her cheeks flamed and she'd stopped looking at him.

"If I'm still here." Her voice wavered.

In passing, Jackson paused long enough to lightly pat her shoulder. He knew better than to offer a hug the way he had after her fright in the cemetery, but he desperately wanted her to know he accepted her, just as she was.

Subconsciously, he had already determined her innocence—although he wasn't free to say so. In a way, that made the situation worse. Not only was Nicki Johnson clueless about how he felt, she didn't deserve to be under siege. And that was precisely what was going on. Nicki was standing firm against unseen forces bent on harming her, and there was nothing anybody could do to stop the onslaught, except find the culprits and send them to jail.

It was Jackson's fondest hope that he would be instrumental in doing just that.

A sense of melancholy kept nibbling away at Nicki's bright morning mood. She usually greeted each new day with enthusiasm and, standing in the lovely, modern kitchen, cooking for two appreciative men, had only added to her joy. Until Jackson had brought up Arianna, that is.

She followed the K-9 officer out onto the porch

and watered her potted geraniums while she watched him briefly exercise Titan before going back inside. The big, black Lab was so full of life, so happy with the slightest praise, Nicki actually envied him.

She could just imagine the look on Jackson's face if she ever admitted she was jealous of the affection he gave his dog! Yet, she was. It was a family thing, a belonging thing. Harold and Jackson and Titan were a tight-knit unit. They cared about each other and it showed. A lot.

Which pointed out the fact that she remained an outsider. She felt like a child looking in the window of a candy store and yearning to taste the sweetness borne of fitting in.

Nicki sighed. She had given her life to Christ and knew He accepted her. So did Pastor Eaton, and probably most of his congregation. Yet, Nicki continued to feel as if she were standing separate. There was a big difference between being a part of a large, impersonal group as opposed to being welcomed by a few individuals who knew your deepest secrets and loved you, anyway.

Perhaps that was what Arianna had been searching for, too, when she'd gotten involved with such bloodthirsty criminals.

Pensive, Nicki leaned against one of the carved porch posts. Titan had been busy sniffing a small patch of scraggly lawn while Harold tended to chores in the barn. Jackson was back inside, dressing for work.

The dog unexpectedly galloped onto the porch and nudged her hand with his nose.

"Yes, I do need a buddy," she crooned, wiggling her fingers behind his ears. "You know that, don't you?"

Instead of continuing to pant and wag his tail, Titan shied away.

"What is it, boy? What's the matter?"

Nicki took a step toward him. He took two steps back. "Titan? It's me. We're friends. Don't you remember?"

The dog cringed, put his tail between his legs and left the porch.

Nicki followed, concerned. "Titan?"

He crept farther away from her, slinking as if he were trying to make himself invisible.

She stopped on the lawn. Watched. Waited to see what he'd do next.

To her horror, the dog approached the ranch truck, the same vehicle they had all ridden in the night before, and plopped into a sitting position next to one set of rear, dual wheels.

His ears were pinned back, his body was trembling.

There was no doubt in Nicki's mind. Titan had just found another bomb!

TWELVE

Jackson was buckling on the belt that held his holster when he heard Nicki start to shriek. She sounded more frantic and panicky this morning than she had when she'd fallen over the disinterred corpse the night before.

He hit the living room at a run and straight-armed the screen door, taking in the entire scene in a flash.

Nicki was bent over, tugging on Titan's collar to force him to go with her. The dog was balking. All four paws slid along the ground, leaving ruts in the gravel.

"What are you doing? Let him go!" Jackson shouted at her.

When she lifted her gaze to his, he saw sheer terror. Her blue eyes were wide, her lips parted, her skin pale.

She made several failed attempts to speak before she finally managed to say, *"Bomb!"*

"Where?"

"Truck."

"How do you know?" By this time, Jackson had reached her side. He snapped a leash on the dog's collar and took command. With one arm around Nicki and the other controlling Titan, he hurried them away.

Harold met them at the door to the barn. "What's all the yelling out here? You two are scarin' the chickens right off their nests."

"Nicki says Titan alerted," Jackson explained as he passed both his charges to the older man. "You stay put with them. I'll call Boomer and get the bomb squad out here to check the truck."

"If that's where the explosive is supposed to be, I reckon I'll back up a tad more," Harold said, slipping an arm around Nicki's shoulders. "Come on. We'll go into the barn."

She hesitated, twisting away. "No. I want to stay right here."

"Then think of me and the dog," Harold reasoned. "We need to take cover, just in case."

"But...Jackson."

"He knows what he's doing. He's a pro, remember?"

Listening to their conversation as he walked away, Jackson wondered if his uncle was giving him too much credit. He was certainly encountering a lot of glitches, lately. Of course it would help if he knew who his adversaries were. Since the perps had no real names, other than those who were deceased, it was difficult to know what kinds of precautions to take.

Danger had obviously followed Nicki to the ranch, he realized with dismay. Slade had probably figured as much when he'd suggested hiring her in the first place. So, what now?

Jackson kept his distance from the suspected explosives as he reported the situation to dispatch by phone. One important question was whether the bomb was rigged to go off when he started to drive, or triggered remotely to better choose its victims. Either was possible.

Whichever it turned out to be, he knew he wasn't going anywhere this morning, and maybe not later, either. As long as a serious threat existed, he was going to have to safeguard Nicki. That was all there was to it. When she had accepted the job at the ranch, she had become his responsibility.

Jackson huffed and shook his head. "Who am I kidding? I've been watching out for her, thinking about her, from the first moment we met."

Which was not that long ago, he reminded himself. So, what in the world was going on? Why did it seem as if they had known each other for ages? And why was there such a strong bond forming?

Yes, she needed help from someone. But why him? Why now? And why was he getting the idea that divine guidance was influencing him? It had been a long time since he'd felt that kind of unquestionable connection to his faith, to his Lord.

Perhaps this was God's way of helping him transition back into the life he had once enjoyed. He had left the military of his own free will, yet he knew in his heart that Titan wasn't the only one who suffered from disturbing combat memories. The difference between him and the traumatized dog was that he had been able to mask his occasional uneasiness while Titan couldn't.

There were many former soldiers coping with far worse emotional scars, Jackson knew. Men and women who might never feel safe again, no matter where they were or what they were doing. He was thankful that his psyche was still fairly intact, but he also feared that if he failed here, if he failed to safeguard Nicolette Johnson, he might never get over it.

"That's not the real problem," he muttered, pacing the yard and keeping an eye on the truck from a distance. "It's not all about me. It's about her. And that baby."

The basic truth of those affirmations hit him squarely in the gut. The woman was practically a stranger, and her child wasn't his. Yet, he already sensed an emotional attachment. To them both.

He glanced toward the barn. Harold must have closed the bay doors just in case something went wrong. That made sense. However, it also meant that Jackson could no longer personally watch Nicki.

One quick scan of the truck and the otherwise empty yard was all it took him to make up his mind. Boomer and the ATF bomb squad might not arrive for hours, depending on how far they had to travel, and what other cases they might currently be working.

So, in the meantime, he was going to stay close to Nicki. He had to. It was more than a job, now. It was a sacred duty.

Wheeling, he headed for the barn.

Nicki was about to sneeze when the squeak of the door and Jackson's sudden appearance startled it out of her. "Whoa! You scared me."

"Sorry. I wanted you to know that the bomb squad has been notified. Are you okay?"

She had pressed her index finger across her upper lip directly under her nose. "Allergies, I guess. Must be the hay. Do we have to stay out here?"

"I suppose not." He looked to Titan. "I'll take

the dog and do a sweep of the yard and house, then we'll talk about relocating."

"Check the house first, will you?" she asked with a forced smile. "I have kitchen chores to finish."

"I hardly think that's important right now."

"Maybe not to you. But I'd feel a lot better if I had something to do besides sit in a barn and sniffle." She could tell from his expression that he was still on high alert so she added, "I can't hide all the time. I won't. Besides, I trust you."

"You should trust the dog more," Jackson said flatly.

Nicki saw a chance to lighten his mood. "I was talking to the dog," she quipped. "But you're helpful, too. He'd have trouble dialing 911 with those big paws."

To her relief, the K-9 officer smiled. It was lopsided and wry but it was a smile, nonetheless. "Has anybody ever told you that you have a strange sense of humor?"

"Often." She chuckled softly. "Since you can't go to work this morning, what's plan B?"

"We wait."

"That's what I was afraid you were going to say." She sighed.

"Patience is a virtue."

Nicki sniffled again. "Yeah, well, it's not one

of mine." She gestured toward the half-open door. "Please? Check for me? I want to go back to the house."

"What's the hurry?" Jackson was scowling and staring at her as if trying to read her mind.

"Nothing nefarious, if that's what you're getting at," she insisted. "I feel more at home in a kitchen, that's all. I don't like all this open space."

Harold piped up. "She's scared of chickens, too."

"What?"

It was Nicki's turn to frown. "They startled me, that's all. How was I to know they roosted all over the barn and were so territorial?"

"You have a lot more serious things to worry about than them," Jackson said soberly. "All right. Nobody can get in or out of here without us seeing them now that it's daylight. If Titan doesn't find anything else wrong, we'll all go back to the house. Harold and I can take turns standing guard from there."

His no-nonsense approach made Nicki shiver. She wrapped her arms around herself and nodded agreement. This mess was all her fault. It had to be, even though she had no idea what was going on. The earlier attacks had been directed at her and these later ones probably were, too, although she didn't know why anybody would put a bomb in the ranch truck when they could just as easily have targeted her personal car.

To eliminate my guardian, she realized with chagrin. Getting rid of Jackson would leave her with one less person to champion her cause, and protect her from whoever they sent next. Murke had been the first, the phone threats and flower bomb had been second. And, chances were, the shot fired at the police car had been the third— not to mention any other times when she might have escaped without even knowing she was under attack, such as from the shadow behind the truck stop that had scared her silly.

And then there was this morning. The threats weren't going to stop. Not even out here where she'd thought she'd be safe.

Tears briefly clouded her vision before she blinked them away, and lifted her chin to affirm resolve. They were not going to beat her. Not now. Not ever. She wasn't alone anymore. God was looking after her. After all, He had sent Jackson, Harold and Titan. What more could she ask? What more could she possibly need?

Jackson was leading his dog out the barn door when she called after him. "One more thing."

He turned. "What?"

"My lessons. Remember? You said you'd teach me to shoot." She let her smile spread as encouragement. "I think it's high time I learned how to protect *myself*."

Behind her, she heard the older man groan. "She'll shoot herself in the leg."

"I will not," Nicki insisted. "Well, how about it? Can we start before the bomb guys get here?"

"If that's what you want," Jackson said in parting.

Nicki whirled to face Harold. "What makes you think I'll be careless? I won't, you know."

"That's what all novices say until they actually hold a firearm in their hands and have to watch every movement, every second. It's not like taking piano lessons or learning to ride a bike. You can never let down your guard. Never."

"Good," she said, meaning it fully. "Because if I aim at anything, I intend to be able to hit it."

"Even a person?"

She rested a hand at her waist, palm open, to unconsciously cradle her unborn child. "If they threatened my family, I think I could act to protect them," she said. "It has to be better to be able to defend yourself than to have to wait for help to arrive that may come too late." Pausing, she glanced at the door. "Like the bomb squad."

"Gotta agree with you there," Harold said. "Just don't get careless. That's all I ask."

Sober and thoughtful, Nicki agreed. "I won't. If I could have chosen my relatives instead of getting stuck with a criminal cousin, I wouldn't have to learn to shoot in the first place."

"That is where it all leads back to, isn't it?" the older man asked.

"Yes." Nicki had run out of arguments, good or bad. "It has to be because of Arianna. And whatever that code was that she mentioned before she died, I sure wish I could turn it over to the police and simplify my life."

Shivering, she added, "Before more people die for nothing."

Jackson took his time inspecting the ranch house and grounds. It was amazing that Titan had alerted to the tampering with the truck in the first place. Normally, working dogs knew when they were on or off duty, and behaved like the family pet when they weren't wearing their official K-9 gear. Titan's consisted of a Kevlar vest as well as a harness and leash, although if he'd stuck his big, wet nose into a bomb and it had exploded, the vest wouldn't have saved his life. Nothing would.

Finishing with the house and its environs, Jackson praised his canine partner and returned with him to the barn.

He almost burst into laughter when he saw what Harold and Nicki were doing. The older man had grabbed a hen by its spindly legs to hold it still and Nicki was tentatively touching its black-and-white, mottled feathers. The hen wasn't acting particularly happy about being held, but at least she wasn't trying to peck anybody. Yet. One look at Titan approaching sent her into a frenzy of beating wings and loud squawking.

Nicki jumped back. "Whoa. I guess she thinks the dog is a predator."

"Something like that." Jackson couldn't help grinning. "Suppose you two quit playing with that chicken and come back to the house with me? I can give Nicki a crash course in gun safety while we wait for the bomb squad."

"And I can start fixing lunch after that," she replied, eyeing the still-ruffled feathers of the hen she'd been touching. "I'm glad we're not having fried chicken. I don't think my new friend would like that."

"I'd never tell," Jackson assured her. He stood at the doorway, rechecked the empty yard, then drew his gun and motioned for his charges to proceed. "Go ahead. I'll cover you."

Nicki made a face. "I'm starting to feel like one of those mechanical rabbits in a shooting gallery. Run this way and duck, run back that way and duck, then turn around and do it all over again."

"This, too, shall pass," Harold said, cupping her elbow while his nephew and Titan stood guard.

"I have to confess, I haven't been a Christian

long enough to know a lot of verses, but that sounds biblical."

"I have my spiritual moments," Harold confided. "Do you go to church regularly?"

"Yes. But under the circumstances, I don't think it would be fair to endanger anyone there by sticking to my normal schedule, do you?"

"Don't worry," Jackson said over his shoulder as she passed behind him. "We'll get this problem of yours solved, and you can start living a normal life again. I promise."

"When?"

"I don't know."

He gritted his teeth, wishing he could give her a more definitive answer. There was none. Nobody knew how long it would be before whoever was targeting Nicki got tired of the so-called game and quit—or unearthed the information she was supposed to be hiding, and no longer needed to harass her for it.

There had to be something they were not seeing—some clue or hint they had missed. Because if there wasn't, there was no way he could ever hope to guarantee her future safety—not to mention that of her unborn child.

Watching Harold shepherd her through the kitchen door, Jackson felt his gut clench. When all this was over, when he was finally able to think straight, he was going to ask Nicolette Johnson for a real date. And then maybe, just maybe, they'd be able to get to know each other on a personal level without having to deal with outside forces repeatedly trying to harm them.

Or worse.

The way Jackson assessed their present situation, there was no way to tell how much of his sense of commitment was due to his job, and how much might be above and beyond the call of duty. He suspected that he was falling for this victim in spite of his training to the contrary—or his determination to keep their relationship strictly professional.

It wasn't rational.

It wasn't right.

It was simply true.

THIRTEEN

Nicki ended up fixing lunch for nine people besides herself. The ATF crew had arrived to disarm the bomb, and local police were there to secure the area as well as take statements from the three of them.

Listening to conversations in the background as she cooked and served burgers, home fries and sweet tea, she learned quite a bit. First, her cousin had definitely been part of a complicated cabal that was still operating in and around Sagebrush.

Why so many lower-level crooks had been marked for death was an unanswered question, although in Arianna's case, she had died while resisting arrest and trying to kill Valerie Salgado. Apparently her cousin believed the female officer had spotted her leaving the scene of a previous murder—although she actually hadn't.

One homicide after another seemed to be occurring, and they all led back to…to *what?* Nicki wondered. How far back did the influence go?

And how in the world was Jackson or anybody on the force going to untangle the repeatedly lethal web of deception?

She was about to ask about the body they'd found in the cemetery when Jackson's boss, Slade McNeal, broached the subject for her.

"I may ask the new medical examiner to review the original Daniel Jones autopsy report, just in case, but I don't anticipate a problem."

Jackson nodded, and wiped his mouth with a paper napkin before asking, "What can he expect to find? I understood that case was pretty cut-and-dried."

"It was," Slade replied. "Still is. We just want to be sure nothing was done to the body after it was disinterred."

"Do you think there might have been tampering?"

The whole conversation was giving Nicki the willies, and she stifled a shiver. At least she thought she had. When her gaze met Jackson's, she realized that he had been watching her and knew she was distressed.

She managed a forced smile for his benefit. "Go on. I'm interested, actually. I'd never seen a corpse before. It was a shock to fall over him but surprising how well he was preserved for having died so long ago. You said it's been five years, right?"

"Give or take," Slade answered. "I still remember the Jones case as if it happened yesterday. One moment I'm about to read the kid his rights, the next thing I know he's lying dead at my feet from a sniper's bullet." His voice dropped until it was little more than a mumble. "Losing the mother so soon after that was the worst part."

Nicki knew it wasn't her place to contradict a professional, yet her heart ached for the captain. "The papers said that woman—Sierra Jones?— took her own life. It's not your fault. There's no way anybody could have predicted she'd react that way."

"We should have made sure someone stayed with her. I can see that now." A shadow crossed Slade's face. "Back then, we weren't careful enough with survivors. Not the way we are these days."

He was alluding to her situation, Nicki concluded. Was that why everyone seemed so solicitous? Why she'd been offered this job in the first place? That notion did not sit well with her.

Then again, she reasoned, she had desperately needed both a new job and a place to stay. How could she fault the result without questioning God's wisdom in taking care of her needs?

Speaking of which, Jackson had gone over firearms safety with her, and had promised they would do some target shooting as soon as the furor at the ranch died down. Nicki could hardly wait. She wasn't the bloodthirsty type. Not at all. But she was now vulnerable in ways she had never before considered. Learning to protect herself and her unborn child made perfect sense. Whether she could bring herself to shoot another human being, however, was a total unknown.

Picturing herself as the underdog, she recalled the Bible story about a shepherd boy, David, slaying the Philistine giant with a slingshot and a rock. She was certainly up against that kind of uneven contest. Given the greater weaponry available these days, she was glad she'd have more than a pebble in a sling with which to defend herself.

Could she? Would she? Nicki wasn't sure.

One thing was clear, however. As long as she was prepared for self-defense, she'd have a fighting chance. Jackson and his uncle could not be expected to shadow her every move 24/7. She wouldn't want them to even try. There was no telling how long she would remain in danger. What if it was years?

That disturbing thought led her to make a new mental connection. Eyes wide, breathing growing shallow, she nervously scanned the men and women seated around the dining room table.

As if a signal had been given, conversation ceased and everyone stared back at her.

Jackson got to his feet, went quickly to her

side and took her hand. "What is it, Nicki? Are you sick?"

"No. No, I...I was just listening to you all talking about murders and I had the strangest notion."

"Well, let's hear it. We haven't exactly been at the top of our game lately. Maybe your viewpoint will help."

"It's about the body. Is there a chance Daniel Jones's murder was the first?"

Jackson scowled. "What do you mean, the first?"

"First of the bunch of killings you're trying to solve right now."

"What makes you say that? Years have passed between that incident and these latest murders."

"I don't know. Maybe it's silly. It just seemed to me that there was no reason to bother digging up his grave unless there was a connection to all the weird stuff that's been going on in Sagebrush." She shrugged. "Never mind. It's a crazy idea."

"Not necessarily. There were drugs involved in all the cases, one way or another. But if the Jones kid was part of the crime syndicate, why send a sniper to kill him?"

"Because the captain was about to arrest him? Like you said, he was young. Foolish. And undoubtedly more likely to cave under police interrogation. Suppose he was shot to silence him?"

"Suppose they *all* were?" Captain McNeal

added. "That code the Munson woman mentioned could still be the key. If somebody thought each of them had it and was refusing to play along, that person could have eliminated the others in the process of his or her search."

"Oh, that makes me feel *much* better," Nicki retorted, the color draining from her face. "What if none of the victims knew any more about a so-called secret code than I do? Where does that leave *me?*"

"Up the creek without a paddle," Harold offered. "Don't worry. We'll look after you."

Nicki knew her voice was rising but she couldn't help it. "Who's going to look after *you,* then? It wasn't my car they stuck that new bomb under."

One of the younger ATF officers jumped into the conversation. "I wouldn't worry too much about that, ma'am. This device was designed to send a message without loss of life, just like the one from your apartment. If the guy who made it had wanted to kill anybody, he would have used a lot more explosive force."

"What do you mean?" Nicki asked.

"The truck bomb wasn't meant to cause a fatality. If it had gone off, all it would have done was damage the steering and probably cause a minor wreck. If they want to be serious, they'll set up a device like the one that almost killed that Sage-brush cop a few years back."

Nicki could tell from the way Jackson tensed beside her that the young ATF officer had erred. He apparently wasn't familiar enough with the town to realize what he'd done, but the suddenly charged atmosphere in the room was so disconcerting he looked around in bewilderment.

Jackson spoke up. "The case you're referring to involved our captain's wife."

Red-faced, the crew-cut rookie muttered to himself for a moment before looking at Slade and offering an apology. "Hey, man, I'm sorry. I didn't mean to sound harsh or dredge up…" Running out of words, he gritted his teeth.

McNeal sighed before saying, "It's all right," although Nicki could see that he had to fight to continue to appear unaffected. They all did. The story of the captain's wife's death was a local legend. No one had ever been charged with her murder and, according to newspaper reports, the police had no leads.

Tugging on Jackson's sleeve, Nicki urged him to accompany her back to the kitchen.

He was scowling as he complied. "What is it?"

"I had another idea," she said slowly, purposefully. "Everybody knows McNeal shot the Jones kid, right?"

"Yes, but we also know that wasn't the bullet that killed him."

"Right. According to the official record, it wasn't. But suppose whoever set the bomb in the McNeal car didn't believe it? Suppose they were after your captain and got his wife by accident just like Harold suggested?"

Jackson slowly shook his head. "I can't see how. It's my understanding that they checked all those possibilities. If the bombing had been related to the Jones boy's death, I'm sure they'd have found the connection."

"I wonder… Picture what it must have been like. The whole department is torn up because tragedy has struck one of their own. The captain is already in bad shape over rumors that he purposely killed a teenager, and then later his own wife gets murdered. How clear is anyone's thinking going to be under those circumstances?"

"You may have a point," Jackson conceded. "I'll have a look at the old case files ASAP." His gaze drifted over her shoulder and zeroed in on a plate of cookies. "In the meantime, how about serving dessert so I can invite our guests to pack up their gear and leave? It's high time you got some target practice."

Nicki nodded as she picked up the plate and started for the dining room. "Okay. Bring the fullest coffeepot, if you don't mind, and let's get this show on the road."

It occurred to her that she should be the one doing all the serving, yet she and Jackson already seemed so in tune that she hadn't hesitated to ask for his assistance.

Not only was that odd in this instance, it was something she didn't recall ever doing before. Nicki's core values required her to serve others, not be served by them. She was capable. Practiced. Self-reliant to a fault. She didn't need to be coddled or waited on like some frail female who was unable to stand on her own two feet.

Except that's turning out to be exactly who I am, she countered, disgusted with herself for admitting weakness.

Unreasonable self-reliance had been the trait that had kept her from becoming a true Christian for years, and it had almost stopped her this time, too. Being at the end of her rope with Bobby Lee and the baby was the only reason she had seen the light, so to speak.

Astonished, she faltered. Her hands began trembling so badly she nearly dropped the platter of cookies before she managed to place it on the table and retreat.

When Jackson followed her out onto the porch, clearly concerned, she averted her gaze rather than allow him to see how unsettled she was feeling.

He came closer, and lightly touched her arm. "What is it. What's wrong?"

Nicki shook her head, still trying to find the words to explain her epiphany to herself, let alone express it so that someone else could understand.

She leaned into him and felt his arm slip around her shoulders, pulling her closer, supporting her physically and emotionally. "It's about my life," she whispered. "I just realized that the things I did that I thought were so wrong were the very things God used to draw me to Him. It wasn't just about salvation and forgiveness, it was about providing a second chance. If I'd been able to see the future, I imagine I'd have tried to fix everything, and might have missed ever becoming a believer." She leaned her head back to look up at him. "Does that make any sense at all?"

"If it does to you, that's good enough for me," he said softly. "I gave up trying to second-guess God years ago when I saw my buddies die in combat while I escaped. I don't think it's wise to try to overthink divine guidance. It'll make your head spin. Just relax and accept it."

Nicki slipped her arms around Jackson's waist and laid her cheek on his chest, listening to his heart hammering in cadence with her own. A few weeks ago, she would never have dreamed she'd be standing on the porch of a rambling ranch house in the arms of its owner, let alone embracing him this way. Yet there was a rightness about it. A sense that what they were doing was not only appropriate, it was mutually necessary.

The words, *thank you, Jesus,* echoed through her mind, her heart, and she repeated them purposefully. She finally saw that she didn't have to understand exactly what was going on before she gave thanks for it. Nor was she through being deeply grateful for her new friends and new job.

In spite of everything that kept happening to her and around her, she was determined to look on the bright side. That vow made her start to smile. If she could manage to see blessings in the act of tripping over a corpse in a dark, deserted cemetery, keep her head when they were being chased and shot at—her grin widened—and be brave enough to actually touch the feathers of a live chicken, there wasn't anything that could keep her from finding hidden blessings in everything, every day.

Like right now, Nicki told herself, knowing she should step away from her protector, yet reluctant to do so.

Then she heard the approaching clomp of cowboy boots and felt Jackson tense. He thrust her away and held her at arm's length. "You okay now?"

Nicki blinked to try to clear her vision, and

managed to mutter, "Uh-huh," although she wasn't too sure.

"Good." He turned to Harold, literally passed her off to the older man, and went to rejoin the officers left in the dining room.

The retired deputy didn't say a word. He didn't have to. Nicki could see empathy in his expression and sense that he was on her side. The trouble was, she didn't know which side she wanted to be on. Did she wish Jackson was interested in her as a person? Was that what his tenderness had meant? Or should she try to keep her distance for everyone's sake because he was merely doing his job?

Believing she was masking her melancholy, she forced a smile.

"He means well," the older man said. "Give him time."

"I don't know what you're talking about," Nicki insisted.

He rolled his eyes and waggled his bushy gray brows. "Oh, brother. Now I've got two of you playing games."

Nicki knew exactly what he meant. She was also determined to keep from admitting it. "There are no games going on, Mr. Worth. All I want to do is stay alive long enough for the police to catch whoever is after me."

And what about future happiness? she asked

herself. At present, the concept of falling for the handsome cowboy cop was the most attractive option she could think of. It was also one of the most foolish. Despite the risks, she knew that her heart was teetering on the brink. It didn't matter whether or not Jackson shared those tender sentiments. One false move, one unguarded moment, and she was going to be hopelessly, helplessly, in love with him.

As soon as Jackson had made his escape from the porch, from Nicki, he felt more in control. The regular police officers in his dining room were getting to their feet and preparing to leave. He almost hated to see them go because that would mean it would be even harder to keep his distance from his lovely new cook. Not that he actually wanted to. Truth to tell, he wished he was still standing on the porch, just the two of them, sharing a mutual embrace. His problem was a conviction that neither of them was behaving appropriately. He certainly wasn't.

Besides, I'm never getting married, he insisted to himself. That thought came to rest as a knot in his gut. *Married?* He hardly knew the Johnson woman. What business did he have thinking such personal thoughts about her?

Perhaps because she was a family in the making, Jackson reasoned. She was tough and resilient and more than capable of taking care of herself, yet she was also vulnerable in ways that would soon be evident as the baby grew. How was she going to make ends meet when she had another mouth to feed, let alone work while the newborn was tiny?

He supposed she could stay on at the ranch indefinitely. That would probably be best for her. The question was, since he was already struggling to keep his distance, how was he going to cope with having her underfoot all the time?

The captain was speaking, drawing Jackson back from his reveries. "I want you to stick close to home for the time being," Slade said. "If we have any more bomb calls, I'll dispatch you. Otherwise, your assignment is witness protection."

"Yes, sir." He cleared his throat as he shook his boss's hand. "One thing more."

Pausing, the captain waited.

"It's something Nicki said. Remember when she asked if there was any chance that the Jones killing and disinterment might be connected to the current crime wave in Sagebrush? Could she be onto something?"

"That's pretty far-fetched." Slade shrugged as if dismissing the notion out of hand.

"I wasn't here back then. Mind if I look into it?"

"Not really, as long as you do your job and

don't let it distract you. Start by talking to one of our cold case detectives, Melody Zachary. That might save you some time."

"I know her from around the coffee machine, mostly," Jackson said, thoughtful. "Shoulder-length dark hair, kinda quiet?"

"That's her. We've talked about her background before. When she's not at the station, you'll find her at the center for at-risk teens where she's the director."

Still uneasy, Jackson glanced in the direction of the back porch where he'd left his uncle and Nicki. "It's an at-risk cook I'm most concerned about."

"Have you had any luck gaining her confidence so she'll open up to you about her cousin?"

"I don't think she's holding anything back, Captain. I really don't. Nicolette Johnson is no fool. If she thought she could end this threat by simply confessing, she would. In a heartbeat. I think she's as clueless as the rest of us."

"That's unfortunate." McNeal squared his hat on his head and huffed. "Because if you're right and I'm wrong, that young woman is in for a rough ride."

"Clearly, whoever is causing all the trouble doesn't want to kill her. If they did, they'd have used C-4 or something equally as deadly in their bombs."

"Maybe so. Until they're certain she really isn't

hiding the supposed code. Once that happens, if it does, she'll be in even worse danger, and you know it."

McNeal started down the front porch steps, then paused to look over his shoulder. "If I were you, instead of expending so much effort comforting her, I'd let her get good and scared. Maybe that's what it'll take to make her talk."

Watching the other officers climb into their various vehicles and pull away, Jackson couldn't get McNeal's advice out of his mind. *Let* her be scared? That notion galled him. Nicki had already been through hell, thanks to whoever was targeting her. There was no way he was going to stand back and allow anyone to get closer to harming her.

What had already taken place, in spite of his best efforts, was plenty bad enough.

FOURTEEN

To say that Nicki loved her job at the ranch would have been an understatement. Not only did she get to plan meals on her own, whatever she prepared was received with eagerness and gratitude.

She was beginning to settle into the daily routine, and had decorated her private quarters as best she could with a few things salvaged from her ruined apartment. Anything that wasn't either washable or hard-surfaced had had to be thrown away due to the permeating smoke odors. Unhappily, that included the old Bible she'd borrowed from Pastor Eaton. When Jackson had realized how upset that loss had made her, he had provided a brand-new, leather-covered edition.

Now the Bible rested on her nightstand beside an old photo of her parents, ready for her evening devotions. She hadn't known what to call the habit of daily Scripture reading until Harold had mentioned doing the same. One other thing he'd told her was that Jackson, although he called himself a Christian, had apparently given up regular Bible study after returning to civilian life.

Titan had begun following her in and out of the kitchen, much to her delight and her boss's chagrin. The dog came for tidbits and stayed for TLC, both of which she dispensed gladly.

The big black dog's limpid brown eyes, gazing up at her as if he had never seen anyone he adored more, warmed Nicki to the core every time they met. His master's eyes would have done the same, she was certain, if Jackson had not been avoiding her so much.

Oh, he showed up for meals, all right. But he didn't linger in her presence unless they had specific plans, such as more target practice. Her aim was getting good. Too good. Jackson had remarked on it the last time they'd plinked at tin cans out behind the barn.

"Looks like I can't teach you much more," he'd said. "You're a natural. As long as you remember the safety rules, you'll do fine."

"I wish I had a sidearm to carry in a holster the way you and Harold do."

"That's all we'd need. Arm the cook, and we'd never be able to tell you we didn't like your recipes."

"Very funny. I told you, I don't think I could hurt another human being."

"Then forget about carrying," he had snapped

back. "Never draw or point a loaded gun unless you're prepared to use it."

"That sounds so callous."

"No more so than standing there like some sacrificial victim and letting the bad guys finish you off."

"Good point," Nicki remembered saying. Now that she was proficient at shooting, however, she knew she'd feel a lot safer armed. After all, the ranch was far from any neighbors, and there had been times when both Harold and Jackson had been busy with chores and she'd been on her own.

Soon, however, the whole house and yard would be filled with members of the law-enforcement community. She had been making preparations for an outdoor barbecue get-together for two days. Brightly colored paper tablecloths with matching, disposable plates and cups covered long tables, beach umbrellas provided extra shade, and Harold already had a whole pig slow roasting in a pit in the side yard.

The main group of guests would be the K-9 unit and their dogs, something Nicki was certainly looking forward to. She had met a few of the others during the crime responses involving herself, but it would be good to see and meet each dog. She especially wanted to give the injured dog, Lexi, a big hug for acting so heroically during the hostage crisis.

Only a couple of weeks had passed since that awful man had broken into her apartment, shot Lexi and pulled her into this mess. Sometimes, it seemed as if that confrontation had happened years ago. Other times it felt immediate. So did losing Arianna.

There were instances when Nicki still felt guilt for having ignored her kin for so long. And then she'd remember that all her current troubles led back to the cousin who had marked her as a target. Whether the act had been malicious or not, the fact remained that she was still walking around with a virtual bull's-eye on her back.

Sighing, Nicki stirred the bowl of frosting she was preparing for one of the special cakes she'd baked. Jackson had suggested she make more than one kind of dessert, and frosting the white layer cake was the last uncompleted task.

A shout from the rear of the house distracted her. She set aside the bowl and whisk and hurried to the back door. Harold was cradling two watermelons that had to weigh twenty pounds each, and Jackson toted plastic bags of crushed ice.

"I've got the door," Nicki said. "Put the extra ice in the big freezer 'til I see what I'll need. The melons can go on the counter or in the sink. Just be careful they don't roll off."

The "Yes, ma'am" she got from Jackson sounded

rather cynical. Well, too bad. If he wanted a nice party, he'd have to learn to follow her orders.

Cowboy boots clomping on the bare floor as he walked, Jackson strode through the main part of the kitchen, and into the pantry where the chest freezer sat.

Harold gingerly placed the melons in the divided sink basins and stood back, breathing hard. "Whew. One more and I'll have 'em all."

As Nicki turned to watch him go, she noticed a flash of movement off to one side. She frowned. Had something just ducked under the kitchen table?

It never occurred to her to be scared. No one had bothered her on the ranch for weeks, and she was certainly not expecting trouble.

She bent. Lifted the edge of the tablecloth. Gasped. Then she screamed, "No!" at the top of her lungs.

The hair on the back of Jackson's neck stood on end. *Nicki!* He whirled and raced back toward her, drawing his gun as he ran.

There she stood in the middle of the kitchen with her hands clamped over her mouth, her eyes wide and glistening.

"What is it? What's wrong?" he shouted.

She merely pointed at the floor.

He didn't see anything out of the ordinary until he leaned down and peered under the table.

Then, he wasn't sure whether to bellow in anger or laugh. Apparently, Titan had gotten tired of waiting for his usual treats and had helped himself. To a whole cake.

Jackson holstered his pistol and turned on Nicki. "You didn't have to scare ten years off my life, woman."

She smiled ruefully. "Oh, my. I am sorry. I just…"

"You've spoiled that dog," Jackson insisted. "It's no wonder he's getting out of hand. I'll have to practically retrain him if I expect him to turn down treats from strangers the way he's supposed to."

"I'm no stranger. Besides, I didn't give him the cake. He stole it."

"Well, the good news is it's not chocolate so it won't be toxic to his system."

"Wonderful." She glanced at the clock over the stove. "I don't have time to bake another one."

"You should have thought of that before you made a house pet out of my working dog. I don't know who I'm madder at, you or him."

Nicki picked up the bowl of now unneeded frosting and gave it a stir. "Bummer. This is starting to stiffen. Without a cake to put it on, I might as well throw it away."

Jackson's hands were fisted on his hips as he

glared down at her. "Serves you right for encouraging Titan's bad behavior."

"Oh, yeah?"

"Yeah." Scowling, Jackson stood his ground while she slowly approached, the bowl cradled against her ribs on one side, the whisk in the other hand. There was a look in her eyes that he couldn't exactly read, but he was pretty sure he didn't like it.

"You need to lighten up, mister," Nicki drawled.

"What are you talking about?"

"Your lousy temper. You used to be such a nice guy. At least I thought so before I got to know you better."

"Maybe the problem is that I got to know *you*," he countered. Having her underfoot for the past few weeks had played havoc with his emotions, and he was nearly at the end of his rope. Pretending that he wasn't attracted to this appealing, delightful woman was the hardest thing he'd tried to do for a long, long time. Maybe his Herculean efforts had made him a little touchy, but that couldn't be helped. After all, this was his life she had waltzed into and turned upside down.

The blue of her eyes seemed to deepen. He was so focused on trying to read her expression, he failed to see what else she was doing.

She raised the hand that had been holding the whisk, opened her fist in front of his face and plopped a glob of frosting right on the end of his nose.

Jackson was flabbergasted. How dare she! Who did she think she was? This was his house. She was his guest. No mature adult should even consider doing such an immature thing, let alone expect another person to tolerate it.

As he saw things he had two choices: let her get away with the act or retaliate. The smirk on her face made his decision a whole lot easier.

He grabbed for the bowl. Almost dropped it. Reached inside and filled his hand.

Nicki screeched and whirled to flee.

Jackson let fly.

The sticky, gooey missile caught her in the back of the head.

She skidded into the wall and left a sugary handprint while changing direction. Coming at him low she clamped a hand on the edge of the bowl and began to wrestle for it.

Jackson whirled like a quarterback carrying a football and held on tight.

Her hand snaked around him, through the space between his side and elbow, and she managed to get more ammunition.

He shouted, "Let go!"

Nicki refused.

The floor was already slippery from their antics and getting worse.

From behind them came a booming, "Hey!" that brought them both to a halt.

Harold was standing in the doorway displaying a grin that threatened to split his face from ear to ear.

Jackson was thoroughly embarrassed, but his adversary seemed delighted with the entire fiasco.

"She started it," he grumbled, before realizing that making an excuse merely contributed to the childishness of the situation.

"If you two are through roughhousing, I suggest you clean up this mess—and yourselves. Our guests will be here in an hour or so."

When Jackson looked at Nicki, he saw that her cheeks were rosy and eyes were still sparkling. In a way, he was glad they had fooled around like silly kids because doing so seemed to have relaxed them both. It had certainly helped him. He had been so keyed up lately, it was a wonder he hadn't bitten her head off instead of accepting her overture of playfulness. She was going to be a good mother. A fun parent who knew how to enjoy herself as well as manage her life sensibly when she needed to.

He was going to miss those things about her when she left, Jackson realized, sobering.

"I'll take care of what's left of the cake and wash the dog," he said flatly. "You go get the frosting out of your hair and change. Harold can mop the floor. He used to do that before you came."

Looking sheepish and still flushed, Nicki grinned at the older man. "Okay, but I'll owe you one."

"You sure will, Ms. Nicki," he quipped back. "And when it comes time to repay me, remember how much I love homemade cherry pie."

"Good thing this wasn't cherry, then!" Nicki giggled. Passing Harold, she cupped a hand around her mouth and spoke in a stage whisper. "I did start it, you know. And I'd do it again. In a heartbeat."

Jackson shook his head and managed to control his own chuckling until she was out of the room. Then he looked at his uncle, blushed and laughed heartily while dragging the cake-sated Labrador retriever out the back door.

Nicki only owned one summer dress, so her choice of what to wear to the party was made for her. A frilly apron tied high over the waist of the full, flower-patterned skirt masked the tiny baby bump. She felt wonderful. Everyone was so sweet to her. And the dogs were magnificent.

All of them were on leashes except Titan, who meandered from one canine visitor to the next, politely touching noses, sniffing and being sniffed, as if personally welcoming them to his home.

The bloodhound, Justice, lay at Austin Black's feet, yawned and looked as if he could barely keep his eyes open. Austin had invited his fiancée, Eva Billows, and her son, Brady, who was currently using the big dog's side as a handy pillow.

In sharp contrast, the little black-and-white border collie, Kip, stayed alert and never missed a thing. It shocked Nicki to be told that Lee Calloway used the sweet-faced dog to locate dead bodies. Lee's petite, blonde companion, Lucy Cullen, didn't seem to mind their gruesome background a bit. As a matter of fact, she had hardly left her husband-to-be's side the whole time they'd been there. Given the trauma of Lucy's amnesia, back when everybody had mistakenly thought her name was Heidi, Nicki supposed it was natural for her to cling to the man she'd fallen in love with during that ordeal.

Then there was Valerie Salgado's Rottweiler, Lexi. Nicki was doubly glad to see for herself that that dog was recovering after being shot in the hind leg, even though she did still limp.

Nicki paused while refilling glasses of iced tea to pet Lexi's broad, black head and speak with the female officer. "I'm so thankful she pulled through," Nicki told Valerie. "When she went down, I was worried the bullet had killed her."

"You and me both. She still has a lot of physical therapy to go through, but she's coming along," Valerie said with a smile. "How are you feeling, by the way?"

Nicki tenderly laid a hand on her slightly thick waist. "I'm good. Barely any morning sickness." She didn't have to force a smile when she glanced over at Jackson. "I can't believe I ended up with a job like this. Not after all that happened. It's ideal, particularly now. I just hope I can stay awhile."

"Why wouldn't you?" Valerie gestured at her nearly empty paper plate. "This meal is delicious. I can't see anybody in his right mind letting you go."

"I don't know. Sometimes my boss acts as if he doesn't like having me around."

"Or he likes it *too* much. Jackson is a hard guy to get close to. He never has been overly chummy."

Nicki arched a brow. "Really?"

"Yes. As a matter of fact, this is the first time he's invited the whole unit out to his ranch, and I'm really sorry my fiancé, Trevor, couldn't make it, and now that I can see the other kids, I wish I'd brought my niece, Bethany." Her eyes grew misty. "I can't believe how instant motherhood has changed my life."

Touched by the officer's candor, Nicki smiled.

"I guess I have a lot of that kind of thing to look forward to. It's not as if I wanted to get pregnant. Not before marriage."

"I know." Valerie laid a hand of comfort on Nicki's arm. "I didn't plan on raising my niece, either, but since that's the way the Lord led me, I can't argue."

"I hope I'm a good mother," Nicki said, sobering.

"You will be. Trust me. It starts to feel natural pretty quickly." Valerie smiled at her. "And if you need any advice about parenting—" she giggled "—ask somebody else."

Nicki rolled her eyes and laughed. "Thanks a bunch. I'll remember that."

Looking around at the other guests she remarked, "Everybody seems to be having a good time. I'm glad."

"Me, too. Lee's been here before because he and Jackson are old friends. And maybe Captain McNeal and a few others have in the course of duty, but we haven't shared social engagements much. I sort of got the idea that Jackson preferred it that way."

"He can be kind of standoffish. Harold says it's because of his time in the service. Titan, too. That kind of thing changes people."

"Hey, daily life here in the States can do that, too," the reddish-haired officer quipped.

"That's certainly true."

As Nicki continued to circulate and top off iced tea glasses, she paused to ruffle the pendulous ears of narcotics detection beagle, Sherlock. He was the smallest of the canines in the Sagebrush unit, and was partnered with Detective Parker Adams. Apparently, that little beagle could smell dope no matter how well it was packaged or hidden.

And then there was Slade McNeal and his five-year-old son, Caleb. The boy seemed unduly shy, but Nicki had been told that a lot of his timidity was due to the loss of his canine buddy, his father's multipurpose, elite German shepherd, Rio. The poor little boy had been mourning since that dog was stolen right out of the McNeal yard.

Nicki could understand feeling so alone and bereft. She had spent many of her teen years experiencing the same thing. That was one reason why she went out of her way to crouch down and speak to the child.

"I have some cookies in the kitchen if you don't like cake," she offered quietly. "I already gave some to Brady Billows over there. See? Maybe you two would like to play later?"

Caleb shook his light brown curls, wrapped his thin arms around his bent knees and averted his gaze.

"Okay." Nicki tried to keep her voice friendly

and open as she straightened. The child was clearly traumatized, and needed to be left alone unless he made an overture himself. That condition was certainly understandable. Not only was he motherless, according to Harold, he had formed a strong attachment to Rio, so strong that the loss of that dog had proved a serious setback to his mental state.

And now the sky was starting to look like rain. Gazing upward, Nicki was struck by how much the gray clouds mirrored the child's somber mood. Even she, who had been upbeat and joyful throughout the afternoon and evening, was beginning to be subdued by the overcast sky.

As if providing affirmation that the party would soon have to end, rumbles of distant thunder began.

Jackson joined Nicki. "We can move the tables and chairs into the barn if it starts to rain," he said.

"Unless everybody decides to head home." She'd been watching the others and noted that the animals seemed to be getting a little restless. "We've had dessert, and they ate up almost everything else I fixed."

"With pleasure, I might add. You outdid yourself, Ms. Johnson."

"I'm glad it all came together so well. Especially after..." Although she was smiling, Nicki also felt her cheeks warming. "I really am sorry about that silly episode in the kitchen. I never should have put frosting on your nose. I don't know what came over me."

"You were keyed up and worried about a lot of things at once, that's all. The frosting fight helped you relax."

"Then you're not holding a grudge?"

The sly smile that lifted the corners of Jackson's mouth told her a lot more than his words. The look he bestowed on her when he drawled, "Well…" was comical, and totally predictable.

If there had not been a sudden crack of lightning and immediate boom of thunder, she might have laughed aloud.

Instead, Nicki and everyone who was gathered in the yard instinctively ducked and headed for cover.

"Looks like the party's over," Harold shouted as he grabbed armloads of picnic supplies and raced toward the kitchen. "Let's get this stuff inside."

Other guests helped clear the tables, then thanked their hosts, bid them a quick goodbye and ran for their various vehicles. Little Caleb and Captain McNeal were the last to go. Nicki made sure the child had his own plastic baggie of homemade cookies to take along.

The letdown after such a busy day was evident

in Harold. Nicki felt it, too. Pregnancy wasn't such a bad thing, if you didn't count being scared and elated at the same time, but it had brought unwelcome changes in her stamina. Thankfully, the K-9 unit had eaten well so there wasn't much to store as leftovers.

As soon as she had refrigerated the perishables, she went outside to unwind and watch the developing storm. Under the cover of the front porch, she could sit and relax in safety while nature put on a light show that rivaled Fourth of July fireworks.

Raindrops as big as golf balls spattered into the dry yard and beat a staccato rhythm against the roof. Stiff breezes carried the odor of fresh rain, of wet grass, and washed the south Texas dust away in rivulets like cleansing tears.

Leaning back and giving the padded glider a push with her feet, she closed her eyes and thought of all the times when she'd dreamed of just such an ideal place—somewhere secure where there were people who cared about her, a solid roof over her head and abundant food in the pantry.

A deep breath ended in a sigh. "Don't get too comfortable," she whispered to herself. "This place may feel like a real home but it isn't yours. Remember that."

Subdued, she knew that her time here was

fleeting. She also knew how much she dreaded the idea of leaving. Maybe someday, after the baby came and her life got back on track, she'd meet somebody who would share her dreams and accept her for who and what she was, sins and all. It was a far-fetched notion, yes, but it helped her cope…anything but let herself foolishly picture Jackson as a permanent part of her future.

Another clap of thunder startled her into opening her eyes. The flashes were coming closer together now, illuminating the early darkness like a strobe globe hanging from the rafters at a high school prom.

Gray shadows in the distance were distorted by sheets of rain. Tree limbs danced in the increasing wind. Leaves were dislodged before their time and tumbled across the yard.

A door banged.

Nicki startled at the noise, and whirled to see who had joined her. There was nobody there. Not even Titan.

"I must have left the screen unlatched," she mused, turning back to watch the storm.

A gust of wind whipped her hair into her eyes. She raked it back with her hands and stood, deciding it was high time to go inside.

That was when she saw it. Or him. The dark form was no more than a shifting shadow, a morphing shape that might have been a man, or might just as easily been a figment of her imagination.

The harder she peered at it, the less distinct it seemed.

Well, real or not, Nicki was not about to make herself a target.

She turned on her heel.

Ran for the door.

Jerked it open and crashed into Jackson.

She wasn't going to stand there exposed and let someone shoot at her. At both of them.

Before he could say more than, "Whoa," she'd given him a hard push and shoved him back inside.

He may have put out his arms to grab her or simply to steady himself. Nicki didn't care. She slipped her arms around his waist and held tight, unwilling to let go.

"What happened out there?" he asked, sounding nearly as breathless as she felt.

"I—I thought I saw somebody."

When he started to disentangle himself from her embrace she stopped him. "Don't go. Please?"

She felt the change in his posture as he once again pulled her closer and began to gently stroke her back.

His assurance of "You're safe. I've got you" was so dear, so poignant it brought tears to her eyes.

FIFTEEN

A search of the yard the following day had been fruitless, just as Jackson had known it would be. He wanted to believe Nicki had spotted a real prowler, but in view of the storm and the particularly strenuous days she'd spent preparing for his party, he was more inclined to think she'd been imagining things.

That, or the shadow of doubt cast over her was making her so paranoid that she thought she saw a nemesis where there was none.

Yet somehow that theory didn't sit right with him.

During the barbecue, Jackson had heard various members of the K-9 unit asking Nicki leading questions, yet as far as he knew, she had fielded all their queries with ease. At this point, he would just about stake his reputation as a cop that she was innocent.

"Which is what I may have to do," he muttered to himself. It helped to know that Harold believed

Nicki's denials of guilt, too. As a matter of fact, the older man was adamant about her innocence.

"What do you have to do?" Harold asked, joining him.

"Just talking to myself," Jackson replied. He scanned the sodden, muddy yard. "Where's Nicki?"

"Inside tidying up. She's not like me. Once I've filled my belly, the last thing I want to do is fuss in the kitchen."

"I've noticed."

"Well, you take after me."

"Never said I didn't." He started for the barn. "C'mon. Let's go where we can talk privately."

"About the girl?"

"Woman," Jackson corrected. "I don't think they like to be called girls anymore."

"Used to." Harold pulled a face. "I miss the good old days when even your granny answered to a polite, *miss*."

"If I remember correctly, Granny could also shoot the eye out of a wild turkey at fifty paces. I'd have called her anything she wanted."

"You've made your point. How is Nicki doing with her shooting lessons? I don't care if she can't hit the broad side of this barn with a scatter gun. Can she be trusted to remember the safety rules?"

"She's fine." Jackson smiled with satisfaction. "Actually, she's a natural marksman."

"I'd still feel better if she wasn't packing. The last thing we need is for her to get scared like she did during that storm and shoot one of our cows."

"She won't. I've shown her where we keep a couple of loaded guns, just in case, but she won't be strapping any on. With the two of us around, she won't need to have a pistol close at hand."

"Which reminds me," Harold began, "I was just coming out to tell you. Your captain called. He wants you at the station for a briefing this afternoon."

"Did he say what about?"

"Nope. And I knew better than to ask."

"Smart man," Jackson said.

"Well, that makes one of us, anyway."

He scowled and studied his uncle's expression. "What's that supposed to mean?"

"Oh, nothing much. I was just thinkin' about how well you and Miss Nicki have been getting along lately. I don't believe I've seen you act playful like that in years. It was a sight for sore eyes."

"What was I supposed to do? She smeared frosting on my face."

"And you could have just wiped it off and walked away mad," Harold argued. "But you didn't. You fought back like a kid would have. I haven't laughed that hard in a long time. Neither have you."

Jackson couldn't help smiling at the memory.

"It was fun. Embarrassing when you showed up, but fun just the same. What do you suppose got into her?"

"If she was eight or nine years old, I'd say she had a crush on you. Might anyway. You could do worse."

"Do worse for what? I made up my mind a long time ago that no cop should ever get married. You, of all people, should agree with that."

"Why? Because my wife found somebody else while I was out saving the world? Not all women are that selfish."

"The ones I've met are. Remember!"

"Then look at the matches some of your buddies have made recently. Austin and Eva. Lee and Lucy. Even Valerie Salgado and that FBI guy of hers, Trevor…?"

"Lewis. Trevor Lewis. But that doesn't mean I'm in the market for a wife."

"Or for a family? Is that what's holding you back?"

"No…of course not. I know Nicki's baby can't help who his father was." He lowered his voice for fear his words might carry enough to reach the kitchen. "His name is Bobby Lee Crawford. I tracked him down. I know where he went after he dumped her and split. I'm just not sure I should tell Nicki, in case…"

"In case she's not over him? I know what you

mean but don't you think she deserves the right to choose?"

"I suppose so. I just…"

Harold was grinning widely. "You just don't want her to leave. Admit it. You're falling for her."

"Between you and me, probably." Jackson gritted his teeth and shook his head. "But as far as Nicki is concerned, I'm her boss and temporary bodyguard. Period. Understand?"

"Yeah." The older man shrugged. "I get it. While she's in danger, we'll keep her safe, and when the air clears and she's proven innocent, you can step up and start courting her proper."

"Maybe. Maybe not. Right now, my captain isn't convinced she can be trusted, and if I show any bias, he might remove me from the case. I can't let that happen. *We* can't let that happen."

"For once we agree a hundred percent." He pointed toward the house. "Better go return McNeal's call and see when he wants you there. I'll look after Nicki while you're gone."

Jackson knew his uncle was perfectly capable. After all, the man had been a trained deputy, a seasoned veteran of the force. There should have been no reason to be hesitant to leave Nicki behind…yet he was.

That had to be because he had let himself get too personally involved, Jackson reasoned, chagrined to admit it. Still, as long as Nicki remained in the dark about his feelings, she'd be safe enough. And soon, when they apprehended the masterminds behind the drug gang war and the rash of related killings, he'd be free to share his thoughts about their possible future. He had made up his mind long ago that even if she spurned him as a potential suitor, he was going to make a home for her and her baby.

He still felt that way. Nicki would be exonerated and then he would invite her to stay on at the ranch.

Will I tell her more? he wondered. *Will I tell her I love her?*

The crystallizing of that thought brought him up short. He *did* love her. In spite of his many vows to the contrary, in spite of his superior's opinion of her guilt, he had fallen hopelessly in love with Nicolette Johnson. She had shown him a future filled with hope. Just being around her had banished the shadows of his painful past.

Setting his jaw, he hurried through the kitchen without greeting her. He couldn't. Not now. Not when he was still coming to terms with his emotion.

If he looked in her eyes, he knew she might be perceptive enough to glimpse his true feelings.

And if she looked back at him with the affection he'd been denying for so long, he knew he'd be lost.

In his imagination, he was already embracing her, kissing her, telling her how much he cared. To do so for real, before he was free to share everything, would be a terrible mistake. For both of them.

Nicki's day seemed to drag on forever, particularly after Jackson left for the station. She knew he'd been called in, and while she certainly didn't resent his sense of duty to Sagebrush, she felt unusually lonesome whenever he was away from home.

Even Titan's pleasant companionship wasn't enough to soothe her, although she was thankful the big dog's presence hadn't been needed in town this time.

Harold had done his best to entertain her, too. After lunch, he'd even invited her outside to show her how to care for the horses.

"I really don't want to learn to ride," she argued, trailing behind him while Titan followed her.

"Won't hurt you to at least brush down one of the mares. They're real gentle."

"And big," Nicki said in awe as they drew closer to a corral next to the barn. "Really big. I had no idea."

"A Texas gal and you haven't been around

horses?" Harold teased. "What's this world coming to?"

"I grew up in town," she replied. "If I couldn't get around by walking, I rode a bike."

He clipped a lead rope to the halter of a round-bellied chestnut mare and led her out the gate before tying her to a stanchion. "How old were you when you lost your folks?"

"In my teens. Mom went first. That's when I started to hang around with my cousin, Arianna, more." Nicki made a face. "Until I saw her for what she really was."

"Is that when you became a cook?"

"Sort of. I cooked for my father for a while, then went to work doing kitchen prep until a grill job opened up at the truck stop. That's how I found out I was good at short-order work. It wasn't a bad job."

"You're too talented for drudgery like that," Harold said. He handed her a brush, slipped his hand into the strap on a similar tool and demonstrated stroking the mare's coat as he continued. "You should have gone to culinary school to become a real chef."

"Special schooling costs money. I was too busy trying to make ends meet and keep my head above water, so to speak, to even think of getting more education. I learned by doing." She smiled as the brush glided over the horse's smooth hide and the animal's skin twitched beneath her soft touch.

"And then what happened?" he asked.

"I got stupid." Nicki paused the brush and made brief eye contact with the older man before looking away. "It's embarrassing to even talk about, but I suppose you may as well hear it from me instead of through the grapevine. I thought I was in love. I thought Bobby Lee wanted to marry me. I fell for his line that we should move in together and pool our resources so we could save up for a wedding." She huffed. "I'm no kid...I should have known better." She took note of Titan, lying in the shade nearby and panting. "If I'd been smart, I'd have gotten a dog instead."

Harold nodded sagely. Nicki noted that he appeared to be concentrating hard on grooming the mare instead of looking at her, and that helped her continue her story without too much awkwardness.

"Bobby Lee played me like a cheap fiddle. I made the mistake of trusting him and look what it got me."

"Seems to me things are starting to improve," Harold remarked. "At least you have a better job and folks who'll look out for you."

"Until the murderer is caught or whoever has been after me gives up," Nicki countered.

"I take it you still have no idea what your late cousin meant when she mentioned you?"

"Nope. Not even an inkling." She glanced over the mare's withers to see if she could tell whether or not he still doubted her honesty. The kindness and sympathy in his expression was very comforting. "You believe me."

"I do. And for what it's worth, so does my nephew."

"Really? I'd wondered about that, particularly after all those other cops kept questioning me at the barbecue."

"They were just doing their jobs. I could tell they liked you, too."

"It did seem that way, didn't it?" Nicki smiled. "I wish it was as easy to tell about people as it is to tell that Titan likes me."

Hearing his name, the black Lab thumped his tail against the hard-packed ground next to the barn.

Harold chuckled. "Hey, feed me as many treats as you sneak out to him, and I'd follow you anywhere, too."

"You noticed?"

"It's hard to miss. That dog looks up to you as if you were his idol. Come to think of it, you probably are."

"The feeling is mutual. All the K-9 unit dogs

are amazing." She sobered. "I sure hope they find Rio soon. I could tell how much that little McNeal boy missed him. The only times he left his father's side at the barbecue was to snuggle with one of the other dogs."

"Yeah. It's been rough for that kid. First he loses his mother and then the dog he counts on for protection and affection gets snatched."

Nicki's hand rested at her waist, fingers splayed over the baby growing within her. "It's going to be hard to raise my child alone, but I can do it. I know I can. Lots of people do fine as single parents."

"Who're you trying to convince? Me, or yourself?"

"Maybe both. I've tried to look ahead, to plan the rest of my life sensibly and sanely. It's hard. I can't tell what to do or think when I know someone is out to get me." She blinked away unshed tears. "What am I going to do, Harold?"

"Pray a lot. Trust the Lord and the folks He's put in your path to help you out. Take one day at a time. That's my motto."

"Mind if I borrow it?" Nicki asked through a forced smile.

"Not at all. Glad to share." He straightened. "I think we've curried her enough. Stay right there while I go get a hoof pick. I'll be right back."

"Is that anything like a toothpick?" she teased.

The sound of the older man's warm laughter was muted as he entered the barn once again.

More relaxed now that she'd become acquainted with the mare, Nicki slipped her fingers through the strands of long mane and wiggled them. The horse turned her head and sniffed, then blew against Nicki's closest arm, tickling her.

She returned the featherlight touch. A few long hairs, like a dog's whiskers, stuck out stiffly, but the rest of the animal's nose was as soft as velvet and warm beneath her hand.

"Okay," she said quietly, "you're not so big and bad after all. But you're sure chubby. What do they feed you, anyway, girl?"

Running her palm gently over the horse's side she felt a bump, then movement. *Of course.* They had something in common. The mare was in foal.

Soon she would be out of shape, too, Nicki mused. That was a given. And even if Jackson had admired her in the past, as she suspected, he was sure to think she looked funny as her pregnancy progressed.

Nicki sighed. Well, that couldn't be helped. It was what it was. She was what she was. God had forgiven her and had used her mistakes to help her heal. For that she was thankful, no matter what.

Perhaps, if things settled down soon, she'd be

able to find another position and leave the ranch before Jackson started thinking she was unattractive.

And then what? she asked herself. What difference did it make if he didn't like her looks? They had no chance for future happiness when she would be the mother of another man's illegitimate offspring. If she herself could not fully come to terms with that situation, how could she expect anyone else to?

A shiver shot up her spine. Was she going to be able to love her baby the way she should? Would she be a good mother? A loving parent? Fair to the innocent little one who had not asked to be born, particularly if it happened to be a boy who reminded her of Bobby Lee.

That, and only that, had to be her prayer. Not for herself, but for her baby.

And she must stop pining for Jackson, too, she reminded herself. It was fine to look up to the man, to rely on him—and his uncle—for safety and shelter. However, it was not reasonable to think they might someday become a couple. Her traitorous hormones were leading her astray, that was all.

She had read that that kind of thing might happen, that she could be fooled into believing almost anything when her body was so out of balance.

The mare lifted its head and stomped one of its hooves, jarring Nicki out of her contemplation.

Titan jumped up, too. His hackles rose. A low growl rumbled from deep in his chest.

Both horse and dog were staring at the house, but Nicki didn't hear or see anything out of the ordinary.

She tensed, wondering if she should run into the barn to fetch Harold. To her relief, she saw him coming toward her.

"Titan just alerted," she said, ruing the fact she sounded breathless. "So did the horse, I think."

"What did they do?"

She pointed. "They both started looking that way."

"Did you hear a car drive up? Anything?"

"No."

Titan had moved to heel on her left and was standing as if he were posing for his portrait at a dog show.

Harold drew his sidearm. "You stay here. I'll go investigate."

"Oh, no, you don't. If you're going, I'm going."

"That's unacceptable."

"So is letting you go off and leave me."

"Titan will protect you."

Nicki chuckled nervously. "If I was a bomb I might buy that. I happen to know he's not trained in protection like some of the other dogs in Jackson's unit."

"No, but his basic instinct is working just fine. Look at him," the older man said, taking a step forward.

Nicki stifled a gasp. Someone or something was coming around the corner of the ranch house! A man. A rather portly man.

Her eyes widened as she assessed the scene. Whoever their visitor was, he was dressed in an expensive, three-piece gray suit with Western tailoring. His highly polished boots had already picked up a coating of Texas mud thanks to the recent storm. In one hand he held a businessman's felt Stetson and in the other a crumpled handkerchief. Considering his pristine attire, and the way he was mopping his damp brow and patting the sparse hair stuck to his forehead, he looked far from intimidating.

Smiling, the man raised a hand and waved the hanky before continuing to blot his pudgy face. "Afternoon, folks. My car broke down a ways back, and I need to use a phone to call a tow truck. Can y'all help me with that?"

Harold holstered his weapon and returned the man's grin. "Sure thing. You from around here?"

"Close enough. I'm glad I found somebody home. I was afraid I was going to have to hike on down the road."

"You don't have a cell phone?" Harold asked, closing the distance between himself and the stranger.

"Battery's dead," the man replied. "Guess I forgot to charge it."

"Well, don't worry. You can call from the house. Follow me."

"Thanks. I could use a drink of water, too, please. I'm real parched."

Nicki saw both men disappear into the kitchen. Although Titan seemed to still be upset, the mare had settled down.

Bending slightly, Nicki laid her palm on the dog's broad head and ruffled his ears with her fingers. "It's okay, boy. Just a passing motorist. Nothing to worry about."

The dog remained stiff in spite of pausing to lick her hand. She stood with him and waited for Harold to return. What was the delay? How long did it take to make one phone call?

Finally out of patience, she called, "Hey, Harold, where are you?"

There was no response. Nothing. Not even a wave from the open kitchen window where the men should be getting drinks from the refrigerator, although she did hear the house phone ringing.

Nicki was torn. If she stayed out there with Titan, she'd be safe for a while. But then what?

What if Harold needed her? Or what if the businessman had fainted. He'd looked pretty pale and weary when he'd arrived, so that was a possibility.

With Titan at her side, she started for the back door. Climbed the stairs. Opened the screen. And stepped into the kitchen.

Harold was there, all right.

So was the man in the gray suit.

And he was holding a gun.

SIXTEEN

Jackson let the ranch landline ring ten times, then hung up and redialed just in case he'd made a mistake. This time, he let it go until the answering machine triggered.

Frustrated, he punched more keys on his phone and brought up the personal cell his uncle rarely bothered to carry. That call went to voice mail.

Across the desk, Captain McNeal frowned. "Something wrong, Worth?"

"I sure hope not. Nobody at the ranch is answering." Jackson made a wry face. "This isn't the first time this has happened. Between Harold and Nicki you'd think one of them would have the sense to keep a working cell close by."

"I'd expect Harold to since he knows there could be trouble. Not so sure about the girl. She seemed pretty cool and collected during the barbecue, though. Nobody got a thing out of her except polite conversation."

"That's because she has nothing to hide," Jackson countered. "I overheard enough to know you'd asked everybody to quiz her. Now are you satisfied?"

"Getting that way," Slade replied. "Still, there may be some clue she doesn't realize she's withholding. Maybe the Munson woman mentioned it casually, and whatever she said didn't register with Nicki at the time."

"It would help if we had a better idea exactly what we're looking for."

Slade scowled. "Yeah. No kidding."

Listening without continuing to make eye contact, Jackson kept trying various phone numbers. The ones connected to his ranch or his uncle had mechanical responses. The one that was Nicki's simply reported that she was unavailable and had not set up a voice mail account.

Jackson gave his superior a serious look. "I need to go home. Now."

"I agree. Tell dispatch where you're headed and keep us posted." He leaned back in his desk chair and laced his fingers behind his head. "I'm sure it's nothing. Too bad we can't teach your dog to use a telephone."

That notion sat heavily in Jackson's gut as he drove out of town. Titan was at home with Nicki and Harold, giving him one more worry rather than a sense of peace. Since Valerie Salgado's dog had been shot and maimed, not to mention prior minor injuries to other dogs in the K-9 unit, like Kip, he'd been more on edge. He and Titan had survived a war zone. It would be ironic if coming home to the States caused worse damage than the PTSD the Lab was already suffering.

Using his thumb on redial he kept calling Harold's cell. Somebody had to hear and answer eventually.

Surely they would.

Unless something terrible had happened.

Nicki's breathing was shallow, her eyes wide. She knew she was gaping at the stranger, but couldn't manage to pretend that seeing the small, silver pistol in his hand didn't bother her.

Harold was backed up against the edge of the kitchen counter, still armed but apparently convinced that drawing his gun would be foolhardy. She agreed. No one could be fast enough to outmaneuver a bullet, particularly one fired from such a short distance.

The interloper barely glanced her way so she remained motionless, waiting, while the phone in her pocket repeatedly played bars from "Yellow Rose."

Growling, Titan stayed with her.

Finally, the armed man said, "Quiet that dog down before I shoot it, and move over closer to the old man where I can keep an eye on you both.

Turn off your cell and put it on the counter with his. Do it. Now!"

Making visual contact with Harold, she saw his slight nod, so she grabbed Titan's collar to control him and took a few tentative steps to comply. "What's going on?"

"I'm about to get what I came for," the man announced hoarsely. Nicki could tell he had not been faking the physical strain from leaving his car on the road and hiking to the barn, but she doubted he'd done so because he'd really broken down.

Harold stepped in front of Nicki as soon as she closed the distance between them. "Whatever you want, you can have. Help yourself. Just leave us alone," he said with a firm tone.

"Butt out, old man. My business is with the woman."

"Forget it. She's off-limits."

Nicki saw their adversary's eyes narrow as he took a step forward, so she raised her free hand with the cell phone in it to signify compliance as she laid it aside. If she'd thought she could have grabbed Harold's gun and fired in time she might have tried, but good sense prevailed. Even if she did manage to get off a shot, she knew the other man would fire, too. And if he didn't shoot her, he'd certainly wound or kill poor Harold and maybe Titan, too.

"I don't want anybody to get hurt," Nicki insisted. She left the little phone and edged away from her erstwhile protector. "Please don't shoot. Just let me put the dog outside. Okay?"

"Good idea. Then shut the door. Don't try any tricks and nobody'll get hurt." He stepped to his left and gestured at Harold with the short barrel of his pistol. "You. Sit in that chair over there and put your hands behind your back so she can tie you up."

Although the older man did move, it was with evident reluctance. "What's all this about? Who are you?"

"What do you care?"

"It's right on the tip of my tongue," Nicki mumbled to herself. "German-sounding, I think. Luther?"

As she continued to guess, she was late looking at Harold so she didn't see him rapidly shaking his head until she'd said, "I know…it's Gunther. Gunther Lamont. I've seen you before. In church, I think it was."

Harold's moan signaled her that she'd made a big mistake. Of course she had. She was too honest to consider the fact that identifying the armed businessman would not bode well for her ultimate survival. Then again, they had no guarantee either of them would live through this long afternoon, let alone greet tomorrow.

Gunther sidled up behind Harold and slipped the old man's sidearm free of the holster, then tucked it into his own waistband before telling Nicki, "Take that extension cord over there and tie him up. Do a good job or I'll shoot him to make sure he stays put."

"Okay, okay." Her hands were trembling, her fingers felt stiff and unwieldy, yet she managed to secure Harold well. She might have tried to arrange an easy escape for him if Lamont had not threatened him with bodily harm.

Nicki straightened and backed away as soon as she was done. With Harold out of commission and Titan banished to the yard, her chances of escape were slim to none.

"What do you want from us?"

"Just from you, Nicolette. I'm an old friend of your cousin, Arianna. Or maybe you know her the way I do, as the Serpent."

"You're part of all that? Why? You're an upstanding citizen."

"Was," Lamont said with chagrin. "I didn't start out looking for criminal connections—they just happened in the course of some slightly shady business dealings that didn't turn out as planned."

"Then it's not too late for you," Nicki insisted. "If you didn't mean to break the law, maybe…"

"Oh, I meant to. And I'm not done, either. Once

I get the code from you and know where to look, I'll be home free."

"That code again." Disgusted, she raised her hands, palms up, and stared at him, trying to decide if he had the guts to actually shoot anybody. Judging by the way he was perspiring and the way his gun hand shook, it was a toss-up. He might mean to fire or his nerves might make his finger twitch and pull the trigger. The result would be the same.

"Yes, the code. You may as well confess."

"I don't know what you're talking about. I didn't know what was going on when Arianna brought it up, and I don't know now. I swear."

"Don't try to kid me, lady. It's paces from someplace in the Lost Woods, like a treasure map, only verbal. So many steps to the left or right, then another number from there and another after that. Get it?"

"Um, I think so." Her gaze met Harold's for a split second, and she saw understanding dawn. He was shaking his head, trying to talk her out of doing anything without actually issuing the warning in so many words.

Nicki was not about to be deterred. If she kept insisting she didn't know this code everybody was after, this man might be desperate enough to shoot her sooner, rather than later. And Harold, too.

"Let me think," Nicki drawled, pretending to remember. "Arianna and I used to play a game like that when we were kids. It was based on our birth dates and years of birth. I think I actually may have an idea what she was talking about when she mentioned me and a code."

"That's better." Lamont mopped his beady brow again. "Let's go."

"Where?"

"To the Lost Woods, of course. You don't think I'd be dumb enough to take you at your word and just walk away, do you? You're coming with me. If you help me find where the Jones kid hid the stash, I may decide to let you go."

"Jones?" Nicki's voice rose. "I was right? This whole mess started with Daniel Jones?"

The armed man laughed dryly. "That's irrelevant at this point. He's dead, and the secret could have died with him if not for your dearly departed cousin."

"How would Arianna find out? Did she even know Daniel Jones?"

"That doesn't matter. Nothing does, as long as you lead me to the spot I'm looking for." He gestured with the pistol. "Move."

"What about the dog? He may be upset when you try to take me away." She hardened her voice as best she could. "If you harm Titan I will not help you. Period."

"Fine. Go get him and tie him up with the old man or shut him in a closet. I don't care. Just make it snappy. I haven't got all day."

Nor do I, Nicki realized with alarm. She hadn't come to grips with the full significance of this situation until that very moment. She could die at any time. So could her innocent baby.

She squeezed her eyes shut for a few seconds and prayed harder than ever before. Words failed her. Her heart did the asking. All she wanted was to live and to protect the people she cared about. And Titan.

It wouldn't have seemed like such a difficult prayer if she had not foreseen disaster for everyone, including and especially, Jackson Worth.

Yet he was her only hope. The only one who might discover her plight in time to orchestrate a rescue.

As she led Titan back into the kitchen and used his leash to secure him to a leg of the table, she passed close enough to Harold to catch his eye and whisper, "Chapel."

Would he understand? Would he remember their recent foray into the Lost Woods and the shoot-out next to the old church…and put two and two together?

She yearned to say more, to explain that she intended to lead her captor on a snipe hunt in the vicinity of the graveyard. However, if she tried to say more, Lamont was liable to overhear and shoot poor Harold just to keep him from sending help. No. She'd have to be satisfied with that one word and trust the Lord to supply the rest.

I do trust God, I really do. I'm just so scared right now. And so worried about Jackson. What if he comes after me and is killed? What then? How will I go on without him?

That was the moment Nicki finally admitted how she truly felt, how much she cared, how deeply she'd fallen in love in spite of the determination to remain unaffected.

Hints of those feelings had tickled at the edges of her mind for days, almost since the first time she'd laid eyes on the handsome Texan, but she'd attributed them to extenuating circumstances rather than seeing them for what they were.

And now? Now, she was sure. She loved the K-9 cop and she cared nearly as much about his dog and his uncle, although obviously not in the same ways.

The hard muzzle of the silver pistol against her spine triggered another wordless prayer. Another silent plea for deliverance. For a way out of this.

As her thoughts spun and her stomach churned, Nicki pictured herself emerging triumphant. She had always had a good imagination. This time, she hoped her dreams would become reality because those nearest and dearest to her were counting on her to think her way out of this dilemma.

And fast.

There was no sign of life when Jackson skidded to a stop between the rear of the house and the barn. Not even Titan greeted him.

He stiffened, drawing his gun and dropping into a crouch. A mare was tied by a halter rope to a metal stanchion next to the nearest corral. Her head was hanging low, but she didn't seem distressed, other than perhaps being a little weary.

Edging closer, Jackson saw brushes and combs near the horse's feet, indicating that someone had been grooming her. So where was everybody now?

Circling the patrol SUV, he slowly approached the kitchen door. It was closed in spite of the warm afternoon. Something was amiss. He could feel it. Sense it. But *what?*

His hand grasped the knob and turned it slowly. The hinges moved an inch and squeaked.

Jackson froze. He could call out now and announce his arrival, or wait to see what lay on the other side of this door. Since no one had answered his telephone calls, he supposed Harold and Nicki could have gone to the grocery store or something innocent like that…but his instincts kept screaming, *Danger!*

Crouching to present a smaller target, Jackson gave the door a push with his fingertips. The noisy hinges wailed.

He heard a low growl.

"Titan? Is that you?"

The big, black dog barreled into him, trailing half of a chewed leash. The response nearly knocked Jackson onto his back pockets.

Looking past his overzealous dog and ordering him "off," Jackson spotted his uncle. Harold wasn't merely seated in one of the kitchen chairs, he was lashed to it.

With his sidearm at the ready, Jackson crossed to him. "What happened? Is the perp still here?"

Harold shook his head, his eyes unusually misty. "No. He's long gone. He took Nicki."

"What?" Jackson holstered his weapon then severed the cord with quick, strong swipes of a knife blade. "Who grabbed her...and why?"

The older man got stiffly to his feet and spoke while he rubbed his throbbing wrists. "It was some businessman named Gunther Lamont. He took her at gunpoint. There was nothing I could do after he got the drop on me." After describing the gunman down to the littlest detail, Harold began to pace. "I should have known better. He said his car quit out on the road. He looked so friendly, so harmless, I let my guard down and he got the drop on me like I was a green recruit."

"Do you know where he took her?"

"I think so."

Jackson was already on the handheld radio, explaining to dispatch what he'd found and asking for assistance. He said, "Hold on and I'll tell you more," before looking to his uncle again.

"She was talking about a secret code she and Arianna used to play with when they were kids. I don't know if she meant it or if she was making up the story as she went along, but she told me she was going back to the chapel in the Lost Woods. That's all I really know."

"Lost Woods. Cemetery," Jackson shouted into the radio. "Silent approach. Code 3 but no sirens. Got that?"

Dispatch said, "Affirmative. Anything else?"

"Yes. The subject is Gunther Lamont. Heavyset white male about fifty. Dressed in a Western-tailored gray suit. Armed and dangerous. He has a hostage. Nicolette Johnson. She managed to let Harold know where they were headed but that's all I know for sure."

"Captain McNeal says we'll also send Austin and his bloodhound, just in case you need them for tracking. ETA approximately thirty."

"I can be there in half that time. If I spot them I'll leave my cruiser where the approaching units can see it and proceed on foot."

He ended the conversation before anyone had a

chance to order him to wait. He was not waiting for anybody or anything. Not on your life. Or, in this case, on Nicki's life.

"I'm coming with you," Harold yelled as Jackson and Titan raced for the police SUV.

"Follow in the truck," Jackson shouted over his shoulder. "And grab my hunting rifle."

"Gotcha. Be careful, son."

Jackson was beyond heeding any warnings. Nicki had been kidnapped. On his watch—even though he had been called away. This should never have happened. It was his fault as much as Harold's. He should never have left her. Never have gone to town without taking her along.

Titan dived into his crate, and Jackson slammed the door. When so many threats against her had taken the form of bombs, he had never dreamed that a person would show up at the ranch and literally abduct her. Especially not someone as seemingly far removed from crime as Gunther Lamont was. The guy had a financial interest in half the businesses in town, as well as being active in the Chamber of Commerce and several service clubs. A man like that didn't go around kidnapping innocent women. It just didn't happen.

Only it had, hadn't it? Nicki was gone, and Lamont had taken her.

Jackson's hands clamped on the steering wheel,

his boot pressing the gas pedal to the floor as he roared away from the ranch.

Was it possible he had misjudged her? Could she have actually known about a secret code all this time and not confided in him? He didn't want to doubt her, didn't want to even think such a thing. Yet, there it was. Harold had heard her mention a code with his own ears.

Okay. One thing at a time, Jackson told himself. First, he would find Nicki and get her away from Lamont. Then he'd ask her why she'd waited so long to open up about her cousin. It was a fair question. And when he looked into her eyes, he'd know if she was being truthful.

Right now, right here, his heart was telling him that Nicki was every bit as law-abiding as he was. Until somebody showed him otherwise, he was going to trust her.

How much?

Jackson gritted his teeth. With his life.

SEVENTEEN

Long shadows made the Lost Woods seem even more frightening than Nicki remembered, and that was saying a lot in view of the fact that the last time she had been there she had fallen over a stiff, icy body and an open grave.

Her kidnapper had strapped her in with her seat belt, then tied her hands by binding her wrists, making it impossible for her to reach the belt release, let alone open the door and throw herself out. Not that she would have. She and her baby had already come through enough trauma to last the entire pregnancy. She wasn't about to endanger her unborn child's life by leaping from a moving vehicle.

Fervent, constant prayer had been her main objective since this ordeal began. When there was nothing she could do for herself, when all avenues of escape had been cut off, she had naturally turned to the Lord.

Somewhere in the Bible it said to "pray without

ceasing" and she could certainly see the point in doing so. She knew she didn't have to be on her knees with her hands folded to speak to God. Nor was piousness necessary. She simply let her heart, her mind, call out with abandon to her heavenly Father.

Unshed tears blurred Nicki's vision. When she blinked they slid silently down her cheeks.

The man behind the wheel of the silver Mercedes was so flushed she wondered if he was going to have a heart attack. Would God save her that way? Maybe. There were certainly plenty of examples in the Bible of Him smiting the enemies of his earthly children.

Gunther Lamont glanced over at her. "What are you staring at?"

"Uh…do you feel okay? Your face is really red. I'd hate to be in a wreck if you had a heart attack or something."

His chortle was choked and far from humorous, although Nicki imagined he'd meant to sound amused. "I feel just fine. And I'll feel even better once you show me where to look."

"I suppose you brought a shovel?"

Muttered curses were the reply. "Never mind the details. Once I see what I need, I'll take care of getting the right tools." A sinister grin lifted the corners of his lips, his smile finally reaching his eyes.

Nicki wondered why his mood had lightened. She didn't have to wait long to find out.

"You just told me half of what I need to know," Lamont said. "I'd been wondering if they'd used one of the crypts, especially if they were in a hurry. Now I know the stash is buried. Thanks."

She shook her head slowly. The man was clearly deranged, at the end of his rope. Desperate. Although the reason for such great anxiety on his part remained unknown.

Nicki leaned back against the butter-soft leather of the luxury car's seat and took deep, settling breaths. The only way she was going to get through this was to keep calm and cool, particularly since her captor was so close to losing control of his emotions. The way she saw it, the more frantic he became, the better her chances of escape, no matter how critical her situation was.

Irony touched at the edges of her mind. Here she sat, kidnapped and in danger of being murdered, and she had just pictured herself wearing a long, white robe and standing with Daniel in the lion's den of the Bible.

Was that so strange? Nicki wondered. Perhaps the Lord was giving her that idea so she'd know to stand firm and not be too frightened.

She huffed. Yeah. And maybe her brain was playing tricks on her as a method of survival. It really didn't matter which was true, or if either notion was logical. All she was certain of was that she was in deep, deep trouble.

Given those parameters, right now, right here, she'd even have welcomed help from Bobby Lee.

That notion struck her as so ludicrous she had to smile. A guy like Bobby Lee would take one look at that gun and hit the trail for parts unknown. As a matter of fact, he had, with far less incentive. Good riddance. Any lingering affection she might have felt for her ex had vanished when she'd realized what real love was like.

It was personified in Jackson Worth.

Nicki simply prayed that she would live long enough to tell him.

The dirt road into the Lost Woods was rutted and bumpy. Since the recent rain it was more muddy than powdery, so Jackson didn't have the benefit of seeing dust clouds ahead to tell him if he was on the right track.

He gritted his teeth. He had to be correct. The alternative was to lose Nicki forever…and he was not going to accept that. Not while he still had breath in his body.

"Father, help me. Help us. Show me the way. Please, God. I have to find her."

Would Titan track her? he wondered. It was possible since she and the dog had bonded so well. The big, affectionate Lab had not been trained to find people, but he was enamored with Nicki so maybe he'd follow her scent.

Titan wasn't the only one who loved that woman, Jackson reminded himself, growing more convinced by the mile. They hadn't known each other nearly as long as he had known a few others he had thought about marrying like Nancy or Ann, yet he and Nicki had clicked in ways he had only dreamed of in the past. She was more than special. She was perfect. At least for him.

He slowed the SUV as they approached the cemetery. Having been there so recently, he was aware of where to park so he wouldn't be seen, and it dawned on him that he had actually been prepared for this very moment. His prayers had been answered long before he'd even prayed them!

Encouraged by that conclusion, Jackson killed the engine, climbed out quietly and circled to get his dog. Titan seemed to understand the need for silence because he didn't bark, didn't even whine.

"Good boy," Jackson whispered, signaling him to jump down. "Come on. Let's find Nicki."

Confused at first, the Lab circled at the end of the long lead and sniffed the dirt. Then he wagged his tail and looked to Jackson.

"I don't know where she is, boy. But we'll find her. I know we will," he said softly.

In the distance a motor revved, then fell silent.

Praise the Lord. He had stopped his own vehicle just in time to keep from being overheard the same way. Score one for the good guys.

Gathering all but about ten feet of the braided nylon lead, Jackson started down the narrow road toward the chapel and adjoining cemetery. Since there had been so much official traffic through there due to the Jones disinterment investigation, it was impossible to be certain about fresh tire tracks.

Pausing and crouching, Jackson pointed to what he thought might be the ruts left by their quarry.

By his side, Titan put his nose to the ground and snuffled. Then he raised his broad head and sniffed the air.

"Nicki?" Jackson whispered. "Can you find Nicki?"

Whether or not the dog understood was a moot point. As soon as Jackson straightened, Titan took off in the direction they'd been traveling.

A jumble of unspoken prayers and confusing possibilities filled Jackson's mind as he trotted after his canine partner.

We'll be in time, he kept insisting. *We'll save her. We have to.* The alternative was unthinkable.

Dragging Nicki out of the car increased Lamont's labored breathing. She didn't help him by moving easily, hoping that the more he was forced to struggle, the better her chances were of eventually getting away.

"All right. We're here. Now start pacing it off."

"I have to begin in exactly the right place or it won't work," Nicki insisted.

She took in their surroundings, noting that the sun was nearly set. If she could delay long enough for night to fall, the darkness would give her a better chance to escape unscathed.

"Well, hurry it up. We haven't got all night."

Ah, but we do, Nicki thought, continuing to make circuitous advances toward the abandoned chapel as if searching the ground for the ideal spot. *The longer I can stall, the more chance there is that help will arrive.*

Was that a foolish fantasy? She didn't think so. After all, Jackson wasn't planning to stay in town long, and he'd surely be home in time to enjoy one of her special evening meals. Therefore, he should discover Harold soon and learn what was happening from him.

And then he'd come after her, she thought, smiling slightly in spite of her tenuous situation.

Off to one side, Gunther Lamont still had his pistol trained on her. He gestured with it. "Find the right place soon, or I'll kill you, anyway."

Another intonation echoed from the direction of one of the nearby crypts, making Nicki gasp.

It wasn't Jackson, as she had initially hoped. Matter of fact, the voice didn't even sound human as it said, "You're a fool."

Did he mean her? Or was he speaking to her captor? The instant she made eye contact with Gunther Lamont, she knew that answer. The speaker was not only addressing her kidnapper, Lamont was frightened so badly he'd forgotten himself and lowered his weapon.

Should she make a run for it? Was this her chance? Maybe her only chance?

In seconds, Nicki realized that flight would be futile. Not only was there one man coming out of hiding accompanied by a large brown-and-black dog, he was flanked by two dangerous-looking companions in camouflage clothing: one crew-cut and stocky, the other long-haired and wiry, as well as twitchy.

The speaker was slim, taller than the others, and dressed all in black, including a knit ski mask that covered his head and most of his face. The eyes she saw through the two upper holes weren't normal. They were black, too, except they showed little or no white around the pupils.

Meeting that gaze was like staring into two bottomless pits filled with indescribable evil. The man exuded it as if surrounded by a cloud of palpable wickedness that accompanied him as he approached.

Lamont began to stammer. "I've just about got the answer for you, Boss. A few more minutes and we'll know where to dig."

The man in black snorted. "Bah. I don't need her anymore. I've figured it out for myself."

"Are you sure?" Gunther asked.

Nicki heard the fear in his tone, sensed how terrified he was of the man he had referred to as his boss. She stood stock-still, hoping to deflect undue notice, particularly since the "Boss" was so focused on the quaking businessman.

"As sure as I need to be," the masked man said. He raised a dark-colored pistol he'd been casually holding at his side and pointed it at Lamont.

The gray-suited businessman raised his hands in silent plea, then managed, "Please. No. No!"

"I can't abide failure. As my second in command, you should be well aware of that."

"I didn't fail. She was about to..." He never got to finish his explanation.

The automatic barked...and Nicki saw the muzzle flash. Cringing in horror, she crouched down on the ground and saw her former captor crumple as if he were a marionette, and someone had just cut all the strings holding him erect.

There was no other movement in the clearing. No sound beyond the echo of the shot. Birds had stopped singing. Insects no longer chirped.

Nicki dared to peek from behind lowered

lashes. The man in black was staring straight at her. All she could see of his mouth was the slash in the knitted fabric but those eyes—those terrifying eyes—pinned her like a butterfly on a scientist's specimen board.

The Boss turned on his heel and started back the way he had come, the dog at his side.

Nicki could hardly breathe, let alone speak. Her feet felt nailed to the ground, her heart was pounding. And she was so scared, she was afraid she might vomit.

Were they going to leave her? Just like that? After everything Gunther Lamont had already put her through? It certainly looked that way.

She straightened slightly, still trembling, yet beginning to fan a tiny spark of hope.

Then she heard the strange voice again—the voice that was so odd it sounded as if it were being electronically altered.

The Boss didn't bother with explanations to his remaining men. He simply tossed a comment over his shoulder as he left.

"The woman. Kill her."

Jackson pulled Titan closer when they heard a shot and took cover behind the trunk of an ancient, gnarled tree. His dog was shaking, as he'd expected. So was he, at least internally. One shot probably meant a hit, whereas a volley of them would indicate that someone was fleeing, and perhaps getting away.

One solitary gunshot was definitely not a good sign. Not good at all.

He waited a few seconds, then cautiously started forward again, heading in the direction of the sound. Whoever had fired had to be in the vicinity of the chapel Nicki had mentioned to Harold.

That might mean she was the victim, he reasoned, immediately abandoning that notion because his heart refused to accept it. Nicki couldn't be gone. She simply couldn't be. Not now. Not when he'd finally realized she was the right woman for him. It wouldn't be fair.

And how fair was it when your buddies died in combat? he asked himself. *Who says any death is fair?* He, of all people, knew that. He'd seen too many friends killed in combat.

Jackson realized his logic was irrefutable, yet he maintained the soul-deep assurance that Nicki had survived. He had taught her to shoot. Maybe she had gotten her hands on the perp's firearm and had used it to defend herself. The idea might be far-fetched, but it was possible. Anything was.

Pushing forward in spite of his underlying fear that he would soon glimpse her lying lifeless on the forest floor, he kept up a constant, unspoken chain of prayer. Words were inadequate in this instance. Hopes and dreams and heartfelt pleas would have to suffice.

A jumble of voices began to drift to him on the evening breeze. *Nicki?* He held his breath and strained to listen.

It *was* her! She was alive. The bullet hadn't ended her life. But then who had been the target? Or had the shot merely been a warning?

Inching closer, Jackson kept Titan on a very short leash.

The dog seemed to sense the need for stealth because he almost tiptoed, placing each paw without making a sound.

Jackson crept closer.

Nicki was talking. "You don't want to do this, guys. I'm pregnant, so you'll be killing an innocent baby, too, if you shoot me."

Jackson nearly shouted out his anguish. Someone was threatening to kill the woman he loved, and he was still too far away to stop it. How much more time did he have? Should he show himself, charge the scene and try to draw their fire, or might his sudden appearance cause the assassin to panic and shoot Nicki, anyway?

On the other hand, if he delayed too long and waited for backup, what would become of her?

Torn between listening to his head or his heart, he started forward cautiously. He knew what a trained officer of the law would do—should do.

But if there was one more shot, he was going to make a run for her…whether it cost him his own life or not.

There was simply no other choice.

EIGHTEEN

Nicki felt better about her chances of survival as soon as she saw the expression on one of the thug's faces soften. His long-haired, younger partner still seemed bent on following their boss's orders, but she believed she may have won one of them over. That was a start.

"I know I'm not showing much yet, but I am pregnant," Nicki explained, focusing on the older of the two men. "If you've been following this case, you know that already. I haven't hidden my condition. As a matter of fact, that's why I was fired from my job at the truck stop."

The one who had chosen to lower his gun nodded. "Yeah. We did hear something about that."

"Doesn't matter," the other insisted. "It's us or her. You know that. If we don't finish her off The Boss will do us, instead, and then send somebody else after her."

"Why should he?" Nicki asked, struggling to

keep from sounding as desperate as she was. "You heard him yourself. He has no more use for me. Whatever he thought I knew doesn't matter anymore. There's no reason to shoot me. Or my poor little baby."

"She's got a point," the sympathetic man said. "My sister just had a kid and it sure is cute. Why don't we let her go?" He turned his eyes on Nicki. "You won't remember what we looked like, will you, lady?"

All she could do was shake her head. Clearly, the younger of the two was far from convinced. That gave her no better than a fifty-fifty chance of survival.

He raked his free hand through his long, stringy brown hair and raised the other arm, pointing his pistol directly at her. "No dice. I ain't gonna die for some dumb broad. If you ain't got the guts to do it with me, I'll do it alone."

Nicki's eyes widened. The round, black hole in the end of the gun's barrel looked enormous. Any second now there would be a sharp crack of sound and a bullet would speed toward her.

This was the end. She'd lost.

Closing her eyes, she clasped her hands and dropped to her knees in prayer. If she had to die, she was going to do it while talking to God.

At least nobody could stop her from doing that.

* * *

Emerging from cover, Jackson shouted, "Police! Drop the gun."

Instead of complying, the long-haired man whirled and fired. The shot went wild.

Jackson's returning bullet found its mark and the would-be gangster dropped in his tracks. His partner had his hands raised in surrender before the wounded man finished twitching.

"Nicki!" Jackson shouted. "Are you all right?"

She jumped up and ran toward him. He had to raise his sidearm to keep from pointing it at her. Thankfully, the surviving mobster made no effort to escape, although he could have bolted at that particular moment and might have gotten away.

Barreling into Jackson's arms, she staggered him. Her face pressed to his neck. Her arms encircled his waist. Tears flowed freely. "Thank God you found me!"

Jackson would have closed his eyes and kissed her soundly if he hadn't needed to keep some of his attention focused on the surviving criminal. It was over. He'd succeeded.

"On your knees. Hands behind your head. Now!" he ordered his prisoner, watching the stocky man awkwardly comply.

"I wasn't gonna shoot her," he insisted. "Honest, man. Ask her. She'll tell you."

Nicki clung to her rescuer and nodded. "He's

telling the truth. He wanted to let me go but the other guy, the one you shot, was going to follow orders."

Briefly assessing the mayhem, Jackson paused. "Orders? Lamont looks dead. Why do as he said now?"

"It wasn't him," Nicki explained. "There was another man. One they called *Boss*. He wore all black, even had a ski mask hiding his face. His eyes were really scary and his voice was creepy, too." She raised her arm and pointed past the chapel. "He went that way."

"When? How long ago?"

"Just a few minutes. I didn't get a good look at the man you spotted in these woods when we were up in my old apartment, but judging by the way this guy was dressed, it could have been the same person."

She glanced past Jackson's shoulder. "Where's Titan?"

"I tied him to a tree back there to keep him out of the line of fire. We'll go get him in a second."

"Then wh-what's moving out there?" she stammered, looking in the direction he'd come from.

"Harold!" Jackson heaved a relieved sigh. "It's about time."

His uncle was panting and gesturing with a hunting rifle. "I figured I was on the right trail when I found the dog. I heard what Nicki just said. Want me to go after this Boss character?"

"No. It's too dangerous," Jackson told him flatly. "We'll wait a few more minutes for backup and then do a proper search with a tracking dog. The guy we're after is probably too crafty to have left a trail this time, either, but he's bound to make a mistake eventually."

Harold turned the rifle on the man with his hands behind his head, and grinned. "Want me to cuff this one for you? I still remember how."

"Sure. I'll keep him covered." Jackson tossed his uncle the handcuffs from his belt, then waited until he was finished securing the criminal before holstering his gun and concentrating on Nicki.

His hands gently cupped her cheeks, his thumbs whisking away the remnants of stray tears. "Tell me you're all right, sweetheart. Please?"

"I'm fine." She leaned against his palm and smiled. "Now that you're here."

Jackson slowly lowered his head and brushed his lips against hers. He hadn't intended to claim a real kiss. Not yet. But the instant he felt her tender, eager response, he changed his mind.

Nicki already had her arms around his waist. Now, she raised on tiptoe, reaching toward the unbridled affection he offered.

He was breathing hard a few moments later when he pulled back far enough to gaze into her eyes. "Wow. I thought it would be nice to kiss you, but I had no idea it would be *that* nice."

"Mmm." Her eyes were misty and half-closed. "Not bad." She began to grin. "Of course, I only had a second or two to judge by. Maybe we should try it again so we're sure…"

"I was sure about my feelings for you a long time ago," Jackson whispered, drawing her close again. "I didn't think it was possible to fall so hard, so fast, but I did. I love you, Nicki."

Her smile waned and she opened her eyes to look quizzically into his. Jackson had anticipated her reaction, based on prior conversations she'd had with him and Harold, so he sought to ease her mind.

"I love *both* of you," he said. "Enough that I've located the baby's missing father for you. If you want to go back to Bobby Lee, I'll step aside."

Nicki tightened her arms around Jackson and met his gaze with self-assurance and resolve. "You'll go nowhere, mister. Not if I have anything to say about it. It's you I love and unless you think we should make him help support this baby, I never want to hear that man's name again. Okay?"

"Very okay," Jackson said, kissing her again before adding, "Why would we want anybody else to have anything to do with our firstborn?"

Nicki was smiling when she leaned back to

catch her breath. "Firstborn? Are you insinuating there will be more?"

"I certainly hope so," he told her. "And kids need a real mommy and daddy. Will you marry me, Nicki?"

"Are you sure? I mean, you aren't asking just because you saved my life again and feel beholden, are you?"

"I think that kind of thing is supposed work the other way around." He chuckled at her befuddled expression, then placed a kiss on her forehead. "Just say yes and stop torturing me, will you?"

"Yes!" she shouted happily. "Yes."

From across the clearing, Harold yelled, "It's about time."

For Nicki, the remainder of that night and the days following became a blur of confusing details and loose ends, although it was good to see that Jackson and the others had truly believed her when she'd told them about making up a fake secret code to stall Gunther until help could arrive. Unfortunately, even knowing all they did about the fallen hierarchy of the crime syndicate, including Lamont, they didn't have nearly enough information.

Important questions remained. Who was this "Boss" that everyone feared and why had he felt the need to steal Captain McNeal's elite police dog, Rio, when there were other dogs that could do virtually the same thing—without causing undue interest from local law enforcement?

The more Nicki struggled to remember minute details of her encounter with the man in the ski mask, the more confused she became. He was fairly tall, particularly compared to the two henchmen he had brought to confront her and Gunther Lamont. And he moved well, as if he had total control of his muscles as well as his emotions.

There was one thing she was certain of. The Boss was a cold, calculating criminal who had little or no regard for human life. Reliving the way he had executed Lamont for his apparent failure still made her queasy.

She chose a peaceful evening at home to ask Jackson a few questions. They were seated together on the porch, making the glider swing by kicking their feet, when Nicki broached the subject.

"What I still don't understand is why any criminal would go around killing his own people. It's crazy."

Jackson threaded his fingers between hers and lifted her hand to brush a kiss across her knuckles. "Mmm. Vanilla. I love your perfume."

"Stop trying to distract me. I think it's a fair

question." She shivered. "For all we know, there may still be murderers after me."

"I doubt it," he told her with resolve. "Now that The Boss, whoever he is, realizes you don't have a clue about whatever it is he's searching for, he'll probably leave you alone. I think the only reason he told those other two to shoot you is because it was expedient at the time, not because he cared one way or another."

"He kills people just for fun?"

"Oh, I imagine he thinks he has good reasons. But that doesn't mean they make sense to the rest of us."

"You're sure my cousin was one of his middle managers?"

"Yes. Arianna was known as *Serpent* and the Realtor she killed, Andrew Garry, was called *Blood.* They were both involved up to their eyebrows."

"Then what about Gunther Lamont? Where does—did—he fit into the picture? He seemed so normal, at first. I'd even seen him in church. What possesses a person like that to risk everything and turn to crime?"

"Probably money, at least to begin with. Then, once somebody is involved the way Lamont was, it becomes a matter of survival."

"And he didn't."

Jackson slipped his arm around her shoulders

and pulled her closer as the swing moved back and forth, lulling them and bringing the peace they both craved. "You're okay and that's all that matters. How are you feeling these days?"

"Fat," Nicki said with a giggle, "and the doctor says I'm only four months along by now. If you're going to give this baby your last name, I think we'd better do it soon—before I start to look too funny."

"You'll never look funny to me, sweetheart. Just set it up with Pastor Eaton. If you want a big wedding with all the trimmings you can have that, too."

"All I need is you—and maybe Harold to give me away. And I'd like to contact my half sister, Mae, and make peace with her, too, if we can find her. Is that all right with you?"

"Fine. We can have a reception out here and invite my whole unit the way we did for the barbecue, only this time I'll have the party catered so you don't have to work so hard."

"Not on your life," Nicki insisted. "I'd love to cook for all your friends again."

"Then we'll celebrate our marriage at a restaurant and you can plan a party here for a later date."

"You don't like my cooking?" Nicki knew that suggestion would flummox Jackson. She wasn't disappointed. He began to sputter and try to find the right words to insist he'd meant nothing of the kind.

She laughed gaily, her blue eyes twinkling in the gold from the setting sun. "Gotcha."

He pulled her closer. Tilted her chin up with one finger. Inclined his head for another kiss— one of many.

Nicki closed her eyes and sighed. They had been through the fires of evil together and had realized their mutual love because of enduring those trials.

This had not been a month she'd care to repeat, yet it had brought out the best in them both. More criminals were out of commission and the future was starting to look so bright it was almost blinding.

As her lips joined with Jackson's and she slipped her arms around his neck, she felt an unexpected flutter in her stomach. It wasn't harsh or painful, simply a sense of movement that caught her by surprise.

She looked up at the man she loved with all her heart and smiled from a joy beyond words.

Her child—*their* child—had just made his or her presence felt for the first time.

They were about to share a new life. In more ways than one.

* * * * *

Dear Reader,

Once again, I'm blessed to be asked to participate in a continuity series with five other Love Inspired Suspense authors. When I heard that there was going to be a series featuring heroic dogs, I knew I wanted to take part. Happily, my editors agreed and here I am.

Dogs, like people, can suffer lasting effects from trauma and abuse. Both my current pets were adopted in spite of having physical and/or mental scars, yet they bring me great joy.

People need lots of love and plenty of forgiveness, too, just as Nicki did in this story. There is no sin too great to be forgiven by God if we will merely believe, confess and ask. The Lord can bring good things out of even our worst mistakes.

I love to hear from readers. Email is fastest. Val@ValerieHansen.com or P.O. Box 13, Glencoe, AR 72539

Blessings,

Valerie Hansen

Questions for Discussion

1. Have you ever seen a working police dog? Is it wise to approach it? Why or why not?

2. Did you realize that the handlers of working dogs take them home and include them in activities with their families? Is this safe?

3. Nicki has made a mistake that will stay with her for her whole life. Is she being realistic to think she can successfully raise her child alone?

4. With no family to go to for help, and being essentially abandoned by her ex, can you see how much courage it takes for Nicki to decide to give this innocent child a chance?

5. Sagebrush, Texas, is a fictitious town. Does it make sense for the police to have all these resources available, or would you expect them to call upon neighboring communities for help the way they do when they need federal assistance from a bomb squad?

6. Various breeds of dogs are mentioned in this series. Why are some better at their specific tasks than others?

7. Part of this story takes place in an old cemetery. Have you ever driven by a place like that and wondered what marvelous stories may lie buried? Have you stopped and walked among the graves?

8. Jackson was in the military with his bomb-sniffing dog, Titan. Did you know that there are retraining programs in which retired working dogs are found homes for the rest of their natural lives? Would you trust such an animal?

9. Nicki and Jackson appear to fall in love very quickly and then marry for the sake of the unborn baby. Is that really smart? Would they be better off waiting and learning more about each other, first?

10. As other members of the K-9 squad meet their future mates and fall in love, Jackson thinks it's like an epidemic. Can love be "catching?" Isn't it normal to want to find the kind of happiness we see in others?

11. When Nicki thinks she's as low as she can go, when she sees no way out of her predicament, she turns to God for answers. Isn't that human nature? Why might the Lord need to use such events? To get our attention?

12. Like weeds in a neglected garden, drugs are the initial reason for the crime spree in Sagebrush. Can you see how one fairly small sin can lead to larger ones just as the seeds from one little weed can take over an entire plot of land and choke out the beneficial plants? What's the best way to stop that kind of thing from happening?

LARGER-PRINT BOOKS!

GET 2 FREE
LARGER-PRINT NOVELS
PLUS 2 FREE
MYSTERY GIFTS

Love Inspired®
SUSPENSE
RIVETING INSPIRATIONAL ROMANCE

Larger-print novels are now available...

YES! Please send me 2 FREE LARGER-PRINT Love Inspired® Suspense novels and my 2 FREE mystery gifts (gifts are worth about $10). After receiving them, if I don't wish to receive any more books, I can return the shipping statement marked "cancel." If I don't cancel, I will receive 4 brand-new novels every month and be billed just $4.99 per book in the U.S. or $5.49 per book in Canada. That's a savings of at least 23% off the cover price. It's quite a bargain! Shipping and handling is just 50¢ per book in the U.S. and 75¢ per book in Canada.* I understand that accepting the 2 free books and gifts places me under no obligation to buy anything. I can always return a shipment and cancel at any time. Even if I never buy another book, the two free books and gifts are mine to keep forever.

110/310 IDN FVZ7

Name	(PLEASE PRINT)	

Address		Apt. #

City	State/Prov.	Zip/Postal Code

Signature (if under 18, a parent or guardian must sign)

Mail to the Harlequin® Reader Service:
IN U.S.A.: P.O. Box 1867, Buffalo, NY 14240-1867
IN CANADA: P.O. Box 609, Fort Erie, Ontario L2A 5X3

**Are you a current subscriber to Love Inspired Suspense books
and want to receive the larger-print edition?
Call 1-800-873-8635 or visit www.ReaderService.com.**

* Terms and prices subject to change without notice. Prices do not include applicable taxes. Sales tax applicable in N.Y. Canadian residents will be charged applicable taxes. Offer not valid in Quebec. This offer is limited to one order per household. Not valid for current subscribers to Love Inspired Suspense larger print books. All orders subject to credit approval. Credit or debit balances in a customer's account(s) may be offset by any other outstanding balance owed by or to the customer. Please allow 4 to 6 weeks for delivery. Offer available while quantities last.

Your Privacy—The Harlequin® Reader Service is committed to protecting your privacy. Our Privacy Policy is available online at www.ReaderService.com or upon request from the Harlequin Reader Service.

We make a portion of our mailing list available to reputable third parties that offer products we believe may interest you. If you prefer that we not exchange your name with third parties, or if you wish to clarify or modify your communication preferences, please visit us at www.ReaderService.com/consumerschoice or write to us at Harlequin Reader Service Preference Service, P.O. Box 9062, Buffalo, NY 14269. Include your complete name and address.

LISLPDIR13

Love Inspired SUSPENSE

RIVETING INSPIRATIONAL ROMANCE

Watch for our series of edge-
of-your-seat suspense novels.
These contemporary tales
of intrigue and romance
feature Christian characters
facing challenges to their faith...
and their lives!

AVAILABLE IN REGULAR
& LARGER-PRINT FORMATS

For exciting stories that reflect traditional values,
visit:
www.ReaderService.com

ReaderService.com

Manage your account online!

- Review your order history
- Manage your payments
- Update your address

*We've designed
the Harlequin® Reader Service
website just for you.*

Enjoy all the features!

- Reader excerpts from any series
- Respond to mailings and special monthly offers
- Discover new series available to you
- Browse the Bonus Bucks catalog
- Share your feedback

Visit us at:
ReaderService.com